*As David Logan investigates
a black-market baby ring in Russia,
he's reunited with the woman he
regretted leaving behind years ago....*

Elizabeth Duncan had finally made it to Russia.

David knew her visit had nothing to do with him—they hadn't been in contact since they'd parted company the evening he'd flown to Moscow. Still, he'd come to this embassy party in the hopes of catching a glimpse of her. Maybe more than a glimpse...

He looked across the room and caught a view of a beautiful redhead in a black gown. The slender straps holding up the dress offered possibilities. He began walking toward her.

"Liz?"

She turned slowly, teasing him first with her profile and then with her whole, incredible face. Those large green eyes and full lips. Heat sizzled between them.

"David Logan," she said, her voice exactly as he remembered. "I wondered if I'd run into you here."

She'd thought of him...and the news pleased him more than it should have.

SUSAN MALLERY

has been a romantic her entire life, so she considers it fitting to make writing romance her career. With a bachelor's degree in business and a master's degree in writing popular fiction, she has an education that satisfies both sides of her brain, which leaves her free to satisfy her readers. Susan always enjoys the opportunity to do projects with other writers. Not only are the stories fun and a challenge, but talking on the phone and communicating via e-mail become play rather than work. Susan makes her home in Southern California (again) where she lives with her handsome prince of a husband and her two aging but still adorable cats. You can visit Susan on the Web at www.SusanMallery.com.

Logan's Legacy

To Love and Protect
Susan Mallery

Silhouette Books

Published by Silhouette Books
America's Publisher of Contemporary Romance

Special thanks and acknowledgment are given
to Susan Mallery for her contribution
to the LOGAN'S LEGACY series.

 SILHOUETTE BOOKS

ISBN 0-373-61384-9

TO LOVE AND PROTECT

Visit Silhouette at www.eHarlequin.com

Printed in U.S.A.

One

"I need a man with good hands," Liz Duncan murmured to herself as she studied the sketch, then the beautiful blond female model she'd hired for the afternoon.

"Don't we all?" Marguerite said as she adjusted the baby she held, then tossed her long hair back over her shoulder. "That's why they wrote a song about it."

Liz tilted her head. Something about the scene wasn't right. The proportion, she thought. With a man holding the baby, the image would be more powerful and evocative. Marguerite's fingers were too delicate, her palms too narrow.

"A song about what?" Liz asked absently.

"Slow hands, honey. Get with the program. If you're going to get a man, get a good one. Make sure he knows what he's doing."

Liz glanced at the tall, slender nineteen-year-old. "I'm talking about work."

"I'm not."

"You never are." Liz flipped through her sketches,

then shook her head. "You can put her down. We're done."

"Sure, boss." She carefully placed the sleeping baby back into the bassinet and lightly touched her cheek. "Thanks for the good time, kid." She looked at Liz. "You really done with me?"

"Sure. I'll let the agency know I changed my mind about the assignment, not that you didn't work out."

"I appreciate that."

Marguerite collected her large tote bag and walked out of the room. Liz crossed to the bassinet and stared at the sleeping baby. The infant's tiny features stirred her heart.

"I wouldn't mind taking you home with me, little one," she murmured. "Too bad this is all about work."

After wheeling the baby back to the nursery, Liz wandered the halls of Children's Connection, the non-profit adoption and fertility center that had hired her to do the artwork for its new brochure. She'd been on manhunts before, but never in connection with her work.

"I should give myself hazard duty pay," she murmured as she rounded a corner and began checking out offices.

She found nine women, three guys over the age of fifty, a hunky guy about thirty, but no strong, masculine types with great hands. Her vision for the brochure was clear—someone holding a baby. At first she'd thought that someone should be a woman, but now she knew better.

She headed toward the exit, thinking the Portland

General Hospital next door might be a better source. Maybe she could find an intern or resident to take pity on her. If her luck held, her baby model would continue to nap peacefully. If she could just—

A man reached the front door the same time she did. He pulled the door open and waited politely for her to exit first. Liz stumbled to a stop as she studied his strong fingers and broad palms. His hands looked more than capable—they looked safe. She could see them cradling the baby, offering shelter and security and the perfect resting place for a tired, trusting infant.

"Change your mind?" the man asked.

"Huh?" Liz blinked at him, then realized he was still holding open the door. Was he leaving?

"Wait! You can't go." Without thinking, she grabbed the sleeve of his leather jacket. "Are you leaving? Do you have a few minutes? Okay, maybe an hour, but no longer. The baby is going to wake up after that. But I've got at least an hour, if you do."

As she spoke, she looked from the man's hands to his face. He was young, maybe in his mid-twenties. Handsome. Confident. Intriguing. Brown eyes regarded her quizzically while a firm, sensual mouth curved up slightly at the corners.

"What?" she asked, aware that she might not have made as much sense as she could have.

"I'm debating between deranged and charming," he told her.

She released his jacket. "I suggest charming. It's more flattering and accurate. I'm occasionally temperamental but almost never crazy. You should hear me out."

"Fair enough." He released the door and stepped back.

As he tucked his hands into the front pockets of his jeans, Liz became aware of a subtle tension crackling between them. Not a surprise, she thought ruefully. Dark-haired guys with broad shoulders were totally her type. Combine that with an air of mystery and an easy disposition and she was almost always open to the possibilities.

"Elizabeth Duncan," she said, holding out her hand. "Liz. I'm a commercial illustrator hired by Children's Connection to do some artwork for their new brochure. If they love my design enough, they'll start using it on letterhead and publicity materials."

"David Logan." His hand engulfed hers. "I can draw a stick figure that would make you green with envy."

She chuckled even as she ignored the slightly crooked, very charming tilt to his smile and the way the warmth from his fingers made her want to purr. She was on a schedule, not just because of her deadline but because her other model—the baby—wouldn't sleep forever.

"So here's the thing," she said. "I have approval for my idea, which was a woman holding a sleeping baby. The drawing focuses on the baby, so we only see the woman's forearms and hands. But when I did a preliminary sketch, it looked all wrong." She tried to look as innocent as possible. "I need a man instead."

One eyebrow rose. "Of course you do."

"I'm serious. You have great hands. The baby is

asleep, so all you have to do is hold her. It's maybe an hour out of your life. Just think, if the people in charge love my design, your hands could be famous. That would have to help with women."

He chuckled. "What makes you think I need help?"

She had a feeling he didn't at all. "Okay, fine. It will give you an edge."

He pulled his hands out of his pockets and glanced at his watch. "Just an hour?"

"I swear. I work fast."

Twenty minutes later David Logan had to concede that Liz was nothing if not determined. She'd collected a sleeping baby from the nursery and brought both of them to a small, empty office with a huge south-facing window. Sunlight poured in—a rare thing for a mid-October day in Portland, Oregon.

"The light's great in here," she said as she slipped off her worn suede jacket. "It's also quiet so we won't be disturbed."

She fussed with the leather executive chair, moving it around until she was happy with the placement. David watched her work, admiring both her ability to focus and the way the light turned her long, wavy auburn hair first gold then red then back to gold.

Liz was beautiful in a fiery, explosive kind of way. Petite, yet curvy, she wore her black jeans skintight and her dark green shirt unbuttoned far enough to show the lace of her bra. Silver earrings dangled nearly to her shoulders.

Her body had been built to drive men insane, but she had the face of an angel. Wide-eyed, full-lipped and innocent. It was a combination that would have caused him to look twice in any circumstances.

She settled him in the chair and then positioned the baby in his arms. He liked Liz's light touch and the way she got lost in her work. He liked her close enough to cloud his judgment.

"You're not comfortable," she said as he held the baby stiffly.

"No kidding. I don't want to break her."

"You won't. Think of this as practice for your future family. Plus, she's too young to judge and I won't tell anyone if you mess up."

"How comforting."

After she'd fussed a few minutes, rolling up the sleeves of his long-sleeved shirt, then unrolling them, she repositioned him again and reached for her sketch pad.

"Stay as still as you can," she said as she began drawing. "Take deep breaths to relax. Don't think about me drawing, instead think about that little girl in your arms. She's so tiny and you're the only person in the world she can depend upon."

David glanced down at the baby. He'd never much thought about kids one way or the other, and he wasn't comfortable holding this one. The only person she could depend on?

"Kid, you're in trouble," he muttered.

Liz chuckled. "So not true, David. You'll be a great dad. Imagine her grown up a little. Maybe three or four.

You come in the door from work and she runs toward you. Her whole face lights up with love and excitement. Her daddy's home."

Her voice and her words created a powerful image in his mind. He could almost see the little girl racing toward him.

"She's seven," Liz continued, her voice low and compelling. "You're teaching her to throw a ball. This is your daughter and there's no way she's going to throw like a girl."

He grinned. "What if I throw like a girl?"

"Oh, sure. *That's* likely."

He studied the baby he held. Her skin was soft and pale, her mouth a perfect rosebud. Tufts of hair draped across her forehead. He wondered who she was and how she'd come to be at Children's Connection. Was she being adopted? Did she belong to one of the employees?

"She's twelve," Liz said. "Tall and skinny and really awkward. You can see how beautiful she's going to be, but no one else can. The boys are teasing her and she comes home in tears. It's been a while since she's wanted to be daddy's little girl, but she's hurt and she crawls into your lap. When you hug her, she feels so small, as if the harsh words could break her. And you want to do anything you can to protect her."

David felt himself tensing, as if there really was a preteen for him to defend. As if this child was his.

"Why the stories?" he asked.

"All questions will be answered later. Just go with me, okay?"

"Sure. I'm about to find those guys and beat the crap out of them."

"I like that in a father. Now she's sixteen and going to her first school dance. She's as beautiful as you always knew she would be. But she's growing up and slipping away and even though you know in your head she'll always be your daughter, in your heart you feel like everything's different."

Without thinking, David tightened his hold on the baby. She couldn't be grown up yet. Not so fast. Not while—

"Done," Liz said, sounding both triumphant and slightly stunned. "This was fast, even for me. I guess I got caught up in the story, too. You can relax."

For the first time David realized his muscles ached from holding so still. He shifted the baby against his chest and moved his arm under her.

"I'll take her," Liz said as she set the sketch pad down on the table and reached for the baby.

David handed her over, then glanced at the picture.

"That's amazing," he said honestly as he gazed at the sketch.

It was exactly as she'd described—a man's hands holding a baby. Simple, minimalistic, yet evocative. There was power in the drawing. The man's hands—his hands—supported the baby in such a way that he could feel the protectiveness and the love. This was not a father who would let anyone mess with his kid.

"How did you do that?" he asked. Was it the curve of the fingers, the shadows? Thirty minutes ago he'd never held a baby in his life. Based on this drawing, he'd been doing it for years.

"I drew the baby first," Liz said as she settled the little girl into the bassinet on wheels. "While I talked, your hold on her changed. I can't explain it, but you just connected to what I was saying. I waited until you were really into it, then drew like crazy."

She looked up and smiled. "The talking thing is a technique I learned in a class. The instructor said the best way to get a subject to do exactly what you want is to make him feel what you want people to feel when they look at the drawing. Sounds strange, but sometimes it works."

She picked up the sketchbook. "They're going to love this. Which means you're officially my model and I need you to sign a release."

The baby whimpered. Liz shook her head.

"Someone is waking up and I'm guessing neither of us is ready to take responsibility for actually dealing with her. Let me run our star back to the nursery, then I'll get you a release form. Oh, and I have expenses on this job. I can even pay you."

"Money?"

"That is the generally accepted means." Her green eyes widened with amusement and anticipation. "Did you have something else in mind?"

Where she was concerned? Absolutely. "Lunch."

"You're on."

* * *

David picked a small bistro down by the river. It was not the kind of place dirt-poor, struggling commercial illustrators frequented so Liz was determined to enjoy every second. The trick was going to be focusing on something other than the man sitting opposite her. It wasn't just that he was handsome and nice and funny, it was the way he looked at her, as if he'd just discovered something amazing about her, and the way he moved his hands when he talked. She had a real thing for his hands.

"Tell me about being a commercial illustrator," he said when they were seated. "Is all your work freelance?"

It was late, nearly one-thirty, and most of the lunch crowd had already come and gone. She and David had the front of the restaurant to themselves.

She brushed her fingers against the thick white tablecloth and stared longingly at the basket of bread. She'd skipped breakfast, more out of financial necessity than a desire to lose weight, and she was starved.

She nodded in response to his question. "No, boss." As the waiter appeared with a pitcher of ice water, she explained, "No regular paycheck, either. I find my own jobs, work my own hours. I'm trying to build a portfolio of just the right work, which means I'm picky about the assignments I take. Times can be lean, but I get by."

"Where does Children's Connection fit into your plans?"

She wrinkled her nose. "I'm not doing it for the

money. There's very little pay. But the exposure and publicity opportunity is huge. Plus I'm a fan of what they do."

He leaned toward her. "Were you adopted?"

"No, but my grandmother was. She was Russian. When her parents were killed during the Second World War, she had nowhere to go. Some aid workers took her in and she ended up in Poland. There she met an American nurse who wanted to bring her here."

His dark gaze moved to her face. "So that explains the great cheekbones."

"Aren't you the slick one? Complimenting my appearance while getting information on my past."

"I have my ways."

She liked his ways. "Enough about me. What do you do?"

Before he could answer, the waiter returned to take their orders. Liz chose a club sandwich, knowing she could take at least half of it home for dinner, and added on a cup of soup. David picked the burger.

"So typically guy," she said. "A burger and fries."

"I have to get my fix while I can."

She picked up her water glass. "Because you'll soon be forbidden to eat red meat?"

"Because I'm heading to Europe in about—" He checked his watch. "Eleven hours."

"You're what?"

He lowered his voice. "I'm a spy and the government is sending me to Russia."

"Oh, please."

He grinned. "It's half true. I really am going to Moscow, but not as a spy. I work for the State Department."

"Like I'm buying that. How old are you?"

"Twenty-five. I was recruited out of college." He held up both hands in a gesture of surrender. "I'm a low-level flunky. Trust me, they hire guys my age. Someone has to do the grunt work."

"An overseas assignment is hardly grunt work." She thought about her nana. "But to see Moscow…" Someday, she promised herself. Because she wanted to and because she'd told Nana she would.

"Have you been?" he asked.

"No. We talked about going, but Nana's health was never great. Not that there was tons of money."

"She must be very proud of you."

"She was." Liz reached for the bread. "She died three years ago."

"I'm sorry."

David's words were a simple, expected courtesy, yet he spoke them as if he meant them. As if he understood loss.

"Thanks." She looked at him. "So what exactly is grunt work for the State Department? I don't guess you carry packages across the border or anything?"

"Sorry, no. But I can probably get you a decoder ring."

She laughed. "I'd like that. Oh, and maybe some disappearing ink."

"I'll check the supply cabinet when I get there."

"How long are you posted overseas?" she asked.

"It can be years. I'll be in Moscow at least three."

Liz felt a twinge of something low in her stomach. Regret? Maybe. She liked David more than she'd liked anyone in a long time.

"What does your family say about that?" she asked.

"I'm one of five kids, so they're used to their children having lives. Besides, my folks are great. They want me to be happy."

Nana would have wanted that for her, too, Liz thought fondly. Happiness and lots of babies. To her grandmother, they were forever linked. Unfortunately, Nana had only had one son and that son had only produced one child.

The waiter appeared with their meals. When he was gone, Liz picked up her soup spoon and glanced at David. "Logan, huh? As in 'the Logans'? The rich computer company family who contribute millions to Children's Connection?"

David sighed. "I believe it's very important to give back." He grinned. "At least I will when I make my fortune. For now, my folks are the generous ones."

More than generous, she thought. She'd heard great things about the family. Based on how terrific David was, she would guess they were true.

"I assume there's no Mrs. Logan accompanying you to Russia?" she asked.

He regarded her seriously. "Nope. Mom's going to stay home, although she did sew my name into the collars of all my dress shirts."

She grinned. "You know what I mean."

"I'm not married, Liz. If I was, I wouldn't be having lunch with you like this."

"Good. I'm not married, either. Although there are two large ex-football players waiting for me back at the apartment."

His mouth dropped open. "You're kidding."

"No, but don't sweat it. They're just roommates."

"Why do I know that's a line?"

"I have no idea. I'm telling the truth. They only have eyes for each other."

After a lengthy lunch they tussled over the bill.

"It's on me," Liz said as she reached for the slip of paper David held. "It's in exchange for you modeling for me. I'm putting it on my expense account, I swear."

David shook his head. "It's my treat. I don't have lunch with a beautiful woman all that often."

He was so lying, she thought humorously.

"I'm on to you," she said as he handed the waiter his credit card. "You act all gentle and charming, but the truth is you're a serious player in the man-woman game. You know all the moves and I doubt you ever spend a night home alone, except by choice."

He winced. "That's unfair."

"But is it wrong?"

He looked at her and smiled. "What about you, Red?" He fingered the fringe on the brown suede jacket she'd just put on. "You play the starving artist, but with really great accessories. I'm going to guess that guys fall all over themselves to stare into those big green eyes of yours." He lowered his voice. "Tell me that you've never done a quick sketch just to impress a potential conquest."

"Not since high school," she protested.

"Any nights alone except by choice?"

She considered the question. "Not really."

"So you're a player, too."

"Okay. Sometimes. Guys are easy."

"Yeah, and nobody gets close."

She stared at him. How did he know that? Keeping men at arm's length was something she did well, and she couldn't always say why. Sometimes she wondered if she didn't want to fall in love or if she was just afraid of feeling too much.

The waiter returned with the credit card and the receipt. David signed it and pocketed his copy. As he put away his card, he studied her.

"I have eight hours until I have to head for the airport. Want to keep me company for the rest of my last day on American soil?"

She had a thousand things she should be doing and right this second she couldn't think of even one.

"Sure, but what about your family? Don't you have to do the goodbye thing?"

"Did it last night. There was a big party." He rose and held out his hand. "Wish you could have been there."

"Me, too."

She stood and tucked her hand in his. His fingers laced with hers.

Liz felt the heat sizzle between them. Her chest tightened, and there was a definite tingle rippling through her thighs. Talk about lousy timing.

They walked along the river until a cold wind forced them indoors, then they settled next to each other in the corner booth of a coffeehouse. The hours slipped by and they couldn't seem to stop talking.

"Everyone tried to talk me out of pursuing this as a career," Liz said with a shrug. "Except Nana, but she believed I could do anything. If I hadn't won the grant right before graduating, I don't know that I would have had the courage to make a go of my art."

She laughed. "Art. That sounds so pretentious. It makes me feel that I should be wearing a black turtleneck and talking about the blindness of the masses. Then I remember *I'm* part of the masses."

David rubbed his thumb across her knuckles. Her skin was smooth and pale. No freckles, no flaws at all. She had small hands with slender fingers. Sensibly short nails, he thought. No flashy polish, no rings. The plainness of her hands was at odds with the dangling earrings and charm-bracelet watch.

But he liked that the same way he liked her quick smile and easy laughter. He turned her hand over and traced the lines there.

"Which one is the life line?" he asked.

"I have no idea. I hope it's the really long one. I have a lot of things on my to-do list and I need time."

"You'll make it," he said with a confidence he couldn't explain.

"Can I have that in writing?"

"Sure."

He stared into her eyes. There were a thousand shades of green in her irises. Even more variations on red, gold and auburn in her hair. With his other hand, he reached up and tucked a loose strand behind her ear. He let his fingers linger, and her breath caught.

"David, this is crazy."

"Tell me about it."

He had to be at the airport by nine. He was already packed, with his luggage in the trunk of his rental car, but instead of thinking about his job and the opportunity he'd been offered, all he could wonder was how he and Liz could be alone together for more than the next couple of hours.

"Tell me more about your family," she said. "What was it like growing up with a twin sister?"

"You really want to talk about that?" he asked.

Her mouth parted. "We have to talk about something."

"Why?"

"Because if we don't—"

Instead of waiting to hear what would happen if they didn't, he kissed her. A handful of customers filled the coffeehouse. Several college students were having a heated debate on the economy, and an old man sat by himself reading the paper. David didn't care about any of them. Right now there was only this moment, this woman and how her mouth felt against his.

She was soft and warm, melting into him as her lips returned the soft, chaste kiss he'd offered. Heat flared, as did desire.

She smelled like flowers, clean skin, sunshine and something that could only be Liz herself. Her fingers clung to his where they held hands. Her free arm wrapped around his neck, pulling him closer.

He released her hand and pulled her hard against him. Sitting next to her, he knew, it would be difficult to touch her everywhere, but he wanted to try. He wanted to feel her breasts pressing against his chest and know the weight of her body on top of his. Need filled him, making him ache. He was hard and ready, and damn it all to hell if he didn't have a plane to catch.

"This is crazy," Liz whispered when he pulled back. "We just met."

He was pleased to see that her eyes were dilated and her breathing just as fast as his own.

"Some things don't take very long," he said. "When they happen fast, they're usually right."

She shook her head. "I don't know. I've never reacted this way. Have you?"

He brushed his mouth against hers. "No. Not even close."

She shivered. "Hold me. Hold me for as much time as we have left. Please."

He tugged her close and draped his arm around her shoulders. They talked some, kissed some and mostly watched time slip away. At a little past eight, they walked out to the parking lot and got in his rental car. He headed back to the Children's Connection parking lot where they'd left her car.

Liz couldn't believe how sad she felt. She'd only

known David a few hours, but it seemed more like a lifetime. The thought of him going away, of never seeing him again, broke her heart.

When he pulled up beside her aging sedan, she turned to him. "Do you really have to go?" she asked softly.

He put the car in Park and faced her. "It's my job, Liz. I've been working for this assignment since the day they hired me."

She ducked her head. "I know. That was silly. If anyone understands giving it all for a career, it's me. But I just…"

"Me, too." He touched her chin, raising her head so she looked at him. "I can't decide if we should stay in touch or make a clean break."

"I don't know, either."

Her chest tightened until it was difficult to breathe. She wanted him—not just sexually, but in so many other ways. She wanted to learn everything about him. She wanted to meet his family and talk about goals and have dates and fights and make memories. If it wasn't completely crazy, she would swear she'd fallen for him.

"Take me with you," she said impulsively. "To Russia."

He cupped her jaw. "You don't know how that tempts me, Liz. We could keep each other warm through the long winter."

It could work, she thought frantically. As a freelance illustrator, she didn't have to punch a time clock. "I could work from there and send my drawings back to my clients," she told him. "It would take me a couple of days to wrap things up here but I could—"

He silenced her with a kiss. The sweet pressure of his mouth told her his answer even as she struggled not to believe him. Her eyes began to burn.

"I know, it's crazy," she whispered.

"But a great dream."

A dream. That was what this was. A beautiful, perfect dream that could never be real. Take off for Russia? For a guy? Never. Not that David wasn't great, but what did she know about him?

Torn between what was sensible and what her heart cried out to claim, Liz opened the passenger door and forced herself to slide out into the night.

"Thank you for a terrific afternoon, David Logan," she said as she fought tears. "I don't think it could get better than this. We should probably keep the memory intact and not try to repeat it."

He nodded. "You're right. But if you ever find yourself in Moscow…"

"I'll look you up. And when you're back in Portland, you do the same."

"Right."

She stared at him, at his face, his eyes. She *was* making the right decision. They both were.

"You're not the one who got away," she said firmly.

"Neither are you."

As she closed the car door, she knew they were both lying.

Two

Nearly five years later

David Logan generally avoided recreational social events at the embassy. His work required more than enough cocktail parties at which he either had to keep his eye on someone dangerous or extract information without the person in question knowing. He no longer found the endless chatter relaxing or fun. Give him a good covert kidnapping or prisoner extraction any day.

But tonight was different. Even though it was his day off, he found himself nodding politely to people he'd seen at events like this a dozen times before and making inane conversation with spouses of staff members. Even as he explained a point of baseball to a security operative from the British embassy, he kept his eye on the circulating crowd. Nearly thirty American tourists had been invited to the evening's festivities, including one Elizabeth Duncan from Portland, Oregon.

Liz had finally made it to Russia.

He knew her visit had nothing to do with him—they

hadn't been in contact since they'd parted company the evening he'd flown to Moscow. Still, he'd come to the party with the hope of catching a glimpse of her. Maybe more than a glimpse. He wanted to look at her, talk to her, find out what was different and what was the same.

Funny how after all this time he could remember everything about their time together. While he wasn't willing to admit she was the one who got away, he would claim a certain interest. He'd never forgotten her. Would she be able to say the same about him?

He concluded his conversation with the British security operative and made his way to the bar. As he crossed the large, crowded room, he glanced toward the entrance and saw a group of Americans standing there.

They wore their nationality as easily as their formal clothing, something that would surprise most of them. His time in Russia had taught David to size up a person in a matter of seconds, and he recognized the well-dressed, well-fed posture of relatively successful Westerners. A few were in Moscow as tourists, some had come to adopt children, and a couple were here for work.

The crowd parted, allowing him a view of a beautiful redhead in a black gown. He wasn't close enough to see the color of her eyes, but he remembered. A vivid green. He also recalled her curiosity, her humor and her drive.

"Champagne," he said to the bartender. "Two."

After collecting the glasses, he made his way through the crowd.

Liz stood talking to a couple in their late thirties. She'd piled her hair on top of her head, which left her neck bare to view. David wanted to move close enough to brush that pale skin with a kiss. Okay, maybe he wanted to do a lot more than that. The slender straps holding up the dress offered possibilities.

"Down, boy," he murmured to himself as he made his way closer. He was acting as if he hadn't been with a woman since he and Liz had parted, but that wasn't true. There had been plenty. Still, none of them had been her.

"Liz?"

He spoke her name quietly. She had her back to him and when she heard the single word she stilled, then slowly turned.

The action gave him a view of her profile first, then her whole face. Humor and surprise and excitement danced in her large green eyes. Her full lips curved up in a smile that both welcomed and beckoned. Heat sizzled, then arced between them.

"David Logan," she said, her voice exactly as he remembered. "I'd wondered if you were still haunting the halls of the Moscow state department."

She'd thought of him. The news pleased him more than it should have.

He handed her a glass of champagne. "Here I am," he told her. "Welcome to Moscow."

She touched her glass to his and sipped. "Thank you," she said. "Oh, let me introduce you to—"

She glanced over her shoulder and saw the couple

she'd been talking to had discreetly faded into the party. Liz turned back to him.

"I guess I'll do the introduction thing later."

"If you'd like."

He didn't care if he never talked to anyone else. Liz was the one who interested him.

"It's been a long time," he said.

"Nearly five years." She smiled. "Hmm, maybe I shouldn't have admitted to knowing the amount of time. Does that sound like I was pining?"

"No. Were you?"

Her smile widened. "Not all the time. And you?"

"When I saw your name on the guest list, I knew I had to come by and see you again."

"Here I am."

He glanced at the elegant dress that skimmed her gorgeous curves before settling just above her ankles. Her large, dangling silver earrings had been replaced with gold-and-diamond studs. He recognized the brand of her watch and the air of confidence around her.

"You've become successful," he said.

"Within my little world, yes. Do the paparazzi follow me around? Not exactly."

"Do you want them to?"

She laughed. "Of course not. I'm simply pointing out that success is relative. I've won a few awards, pleased some well-placed clients, moved up the food chain."

"Good. Still living with the football players?"

"No. It's just me now, which is really better. When those two fought, they were impossible."

She wasn't married. David told himself the information shouldn't have mattered, but he liked knowing it.

"What about you?" she asked. "How's the spy business?"

"I've been working on improving invisible ink."

"How's that going?"

"Great. Only my work keeps disappearing."

"That could be a problem."

David sounded the same, Liz thought happily. Still charming, still easy to be with, but he looked different. Harder, leaner, more dangerous. His dark eyes contained secrets. He might joke about invisible ink but she suspected the truth about his job would make her shiver with fear.

He touched her arm and she felt the warm contact all the way to her toes.

"What are you thinking?" he asked. "You just got serious."

She clutched her champagne glass and forced herself to relax. "You. When I was planning my trip, I wondered if you would be here. I thought about looking you up but..." She shrugged. "It was only one afternoon."

He stared deeply into her eyes. "It was a hell of a lot more than that."

Her stomach clenched slightly. It had been more for her, too.

"Sometimes I thought I'd imagined it all," she admitted. "That we hadn't really connected that way so quickly."

"It was all real."

He moved a little closer. Close enough that breathing didn't seem all that necessary. Close enough to make her grateful that her dress slipped on and off so easily. Close enough that she thought about kissing him and touching him and having him touch her back. She thought about the large embassy and the empty rooms and how they could—

Liz consciously cleared her head and sucked in a breath. Time to regroup.

"So," she said, striving for a cheerful tone, "how's Mrs. Logan?"

He chuckled. "My mother is fine. Busy with her charity work. I'll be sure to tell her you were asking. She was just here a few weeks ago. My parents visit a couple of times of year. It was cold and rainy for their visit, but you've come at a good time."

Moscow weather seemed like a safe topic. "I'm glad. I'm hoping to have time to see a few things while I'm here."

"Looking for a tour guide?"

"Maybe. Do you know someone?"

"A great guy."

David was only a few inches taller than she, yet he seemed so much larger. And safe. She liked the combination of erotic arousal and comfort she felt standing next to him.

"Does he speak both English and Russian?" she asked.

"Oh, yeah. He's also passable in German but he could dazzle you in French."

"I'm not easily dazzled."

"He's up to the task."

"Is he?"

"I promise."

They were talking about more than just a tour of the city, she thought with a combination of excitement and trepidation. "Maybe you could give me his number."

"I thought I'd introduce you myself. That would make it more personal. How much time will you have to see the sights?"

Liz took another sip of her champagne and realized David had no idea why she was in Moscow. Would the information change things? Silly question. Of course it would.

"I have a couple of days until things get complicated," she said. "I'm not here on vacation. I'm with the Children's Connection group. I'm adopting a baby girl."

David's expression didn't change, nor did his body language, which told her she would never want to play poker against the man.

"Weren't you working with them when we first met?" he asked.

"Yes. I did the artwork for their brochure."

"And now you're adopting a baby through them. My family is a big supporter of what they do. That's why my parents were here. Well, to visit me, too."

"How ironic we met last time because of Children's Connection and here we are again, because of them," she said.

"Remind me to send a thank-you note."

She still couldn't tell what he was thinking. He was so cool, she thought. Didn't he have questions for her?

"Do you want to comment on my decision to adopt?" she asked.

He continued to study her face. "It's an interesting choice for a single woman," he said.

"Agreed." She shrugged. "There are a lot of reasons. I'm successful and I can afford to take care of a baby. My work schedule is flexible—another plus."

"Most women prefer to wait for home and husband."

"True enough. I have the home, but I'm not interested in waiting for the husband."

Getting married would mean falling in love and Liz wasn't a fan of the process. In her world, romantic love cost too much and she wasn't willing to pay.

"At the risk of discussing something too personal, why don't you have a child of your own?" he asked.

"I'm sure you don't remember, but I was raised by my grandmother."

"Of course. Your nana." He raised his eyebrows. "She was Russian."

"I'm impressed you remembered." More than impressed. Intrigued.

"It's the spy training. I never forget a detail."

Despite their relatively serious conversation, Liz smiled. "You're still good-looking and charming. I can't believe someone hasn't snatched you up."

"Maybe I haven't been available."

"Their loss."

She meant it. She might not be interested in happily-

ever-after, but that didn't make her any less apprecia-
tive of David's appeal.

He finished his glass of champagne. "Your grandmother was adopted," he said.

"Right. After the Second World War. She was
brought back to the States. She and I used to talk about
her life before—how hard things were. Maybe the seed
was planted there. When I did the brochure for Children's Connection, I learned about their international
adoptions. At the time it wasn't practical, but eventually I realized it was something I wanted to do."

He put his hand on the small of her back and guided
her to a small sofa in an alcove by a large window.
When she was seated, he sat next to her, angling his
body toward hers.

"Was the process difficult?" he asked.

He was sitting close enough to interfere with her
mental process. She had to consciously focus on the
topic to form actual sentences.

"There's plenty of paperwork. I had to go through a
home study and get all kinds of approvals and documents. I had an initial visit to meet Natasha—that's the
baby's name. That was about a month ago. I was only
here for a couple of days. I thought about trying to find
you but…"

"There was a lot going on," he said, brushing his fingers across the back of her hand.

"Right."

The full days hadn't been the only reason, she admitted to herself. She'd been cautious. It had taken a ri-

diculous amount of time to get over David five years ago. She hadn't wanted the distraction of trying to deal with him now.

But sitting next to him—aware of his heat, the scent of his body and the rapid beating of her own heart—she knew that she'd mostly been afraid and with good reason. The man turned her head.

"I had plenty of doubts about the adoption process and what I was doing," she admitted. "Was I crazy to fly halfway around the world to adopt a child? But then I held Natasha in my arms and I knew she was exactly what I'd been waiting for all my life."

"Sounds special."

"It was. Now I'm here for the second and final visit. Depending on how the process goes, I'll be in Moscow for anywhere from several days to several weeks. Then I'll bring her home with me."

"When does this all start?" he asked.

"I'll go to the orphanage the day after tomorrow. Until then I'm free."

He brushed his thumb across the back of her hand. "Is that an invitation?"

She wanted it to be. "Are you interested?"

His slow, sexy smile made her grateful she was sitting and didn't have to worry about mundane things like staying upright and balancing herself.

"Absolutely."

The next day David left his office shortly after ten in the morning. He'd gone in to handle a few pressing problems, then had taken the rest of the day off to show Liz around Moscow.

She was trouble, he acknowledged as he took the stairs to the underground garage. Beautiful, seductive and not for the likes of him. Still, wanting and not having was a unique experience—one he was willing to endure for now.

She'd shown up unexpectedly and the surprises kept on coming. Adopting a child on her own would mean a big change. Five years ago she'd been focused on her career. Apparently that was no longer the case.

They were both different, he thought as he slid into his green Fiat and started the engine..He knew the past five years had changed him in ways he would never talk about. There were still dark places in the Russian Federation and he'd been to most of them.

The drive to the hotel took less than twenty minutes. The five-story building stood on a narrow street, butting up against an apartment block and a private school. David parked, then surveyed the neighborhood. Not elegant, but safe.

The lobby had seen better days. Once beautiful Oriental carpeting had faded until the pattern was little more than a shadow. The carved molding was cracked in several places, but the crystal in the chandelier was authentic and original. The clerk behind the registration desk noted David's arrival but said nothing to him as he took the stairs to the third floor and knocked on Liz's door. She answered at once, pulling back the door and smiling at him.

"Right on time," she said. "You'd warned me you might not be able to get away very easily."

"I was motivated," he told her as he leaned in and kissed her cheek.

She smelled of soap and flowers and female mysteries. Today she wore her hair down and slightly curled. Over her jeans she had on a yellow T-shirt that hugged her breasts in such a way that he knew he would be distracted the entire day.

As he straightened, their gazes locked. That ever-present heat flared until all he wanted to do was push her back into the room, lock the door behind them and spend the day in bed. Naked.

Instead he retreated to the relative safety of the hallway and stuck his hands into his jeans' front pockets.

"You about ready?"

"Uh-huh."

Her smile told him she'd been more than aware of his dilemma, but not how she would have reacted if he'd given in to temptation. He liked to think that she wouldn't have put up much of a fight.

"So what's on the agenda?" she asked.

"How much of the city did you see last time you were here?"

She checked her fanny pack for her key, then closed the door and followed him into the hallway.

"Practically nothing. Between the jet lag and meeting Natasha, I barely functioned. That's why I came in a day early this time—so I could get on Moscow time and be more relaxed."

He led the way to the stairs. "You're adopting a child. How relaxed could you be?"

"Good point. So basically I'm a tourist who knows nothing and has seen even less."

He took her hand in his. "Then trust me to show you Moscow. We'll drive around to give you a general idea of things, then stop at a place I promise you'll never forget."

"Sounds great."

Liz liked the way David's hand felt holding hers. She liked being close to him. Honestly, she liked a lot of things, including the fact that he was a giant, good-looking distraction. Coming in early so she wouldn't be so exhausted during the final adoption process had seemed like a good idea at the time, but flying over, she'd realized it also gave her too much time to think about what she was doing. Not that she regretted any part of adopting Natasha. Instead, she worried about being a good enough mother for the delightful baby.

But with David at her side, she could fill her mind with other intriguing topics and different fantasies. Such as how it was possible for one man to produce so many tingles in her body.

He escorted her to a small green car parked down the street. As they took off, she felt a thrill of excitement. She was about as far from home as she'd ever been, in the company of a handsome man, starting an adventure that would change her life. What could be better?

"Tell me about living here," she said as they turned a corner and entered a busy main street. "Do you have much contact with Russian people?"

"I try to. When I came here I knew a lot in theory, but had no practical experience with another culture." He shot her a grin. "Now I'm practically a native."

"Sure you are. Say something in Russian."

He obliged with a long sentence. She blinked at him.

"Okay, and what did you say?"

"That this was the kind of day meant to be spent with a beautiful woman. Then I said something dirty I can't repeat."

She laughed. "Fair enough. So tell me about the people of this city."

"They're welcoming and warm. Even to strangers. Especially to strangers. When you're in someone's home, there's plenty of vodka to go around, and plates and plates of food. Guests are expected to bring a gift. Residents are fiercely loyal to their culture and their history. Russian brands are always preferred. Oh, and when you give flowers, always do so in an odd number. No one here wants a dozen roses."

"Interesting."

They crossed a wide river and David began pointing out different buildings. There were museums and theaters and more churches than she'd thought possible, each more beautiful than the last.

"The American embassy," he said, pointing to his left. "You were there last night."

"The place to run to if I get into trouble, right?" she asked with a chuckle.

David glanced at her. "Absolutely. Don't hesitate, even for a second. If something happens, go there."

He sounded fierce and she shivered. "Are you trying to scare me?"

"Just keeping you safe. Life is different here than back in Portland. You need to remember that."

"Don't worry. Except for this day of sight-seeing, my trip here will revolve around the orphanage and getting Natasha. I doubt I'll get into any trouble with that."

"Good point."

He continued to drive around, showing her the sights. At last they parked and began to walk.

The June day was sunny and in the high sixties. David had brought her to a tourist area and she saw people from all over the world. She recognized a few of the languages spoken, but not all.

"Do you like it here?" she asked.

"Yes."

"How long are you going to stay?"

"I'm not sure. I've already extended my assignment twice. I could head back to the States if I wanted."

"Do you want to, or is the spy business too good?"

He took her hand and laced his fingers with hers. "I'm into the James Bond thing. It works with the ladies."

"Like you need help there." She glanced at him out of the corner of her eye. "Seriously, David, you're not actually a spy, right?"

"I'm an attaché with the Department of Information."

"And…?"

"And here's what I brought you to see."

He stopped walking and pointed to their right. Liz was about to complain that he hadn't really answered the question when she turned and saw the most amazing structure she'd ever seen in her life.

The building was huge, a mass of colors and different-shaped domes. Parts were familiar, as if she'd seen them in pictures or on television.

"St. Basil's Cathedral," David said. "Built in the mid 1500s by Ivan the Terrible. He was said to have blinded the architects after they finished so that they could never build such a beautiful church again."

"The man earned his title."

"In every way possible."

David led her through the church. She couldn't believe how beautiful everything was, from the flowers painted on the walls to the many icons. Restoration was under way in parts of the church, and she paused to drop money into a box for the fund.

"They'll be intrigued," he said as she finished pushing in a five-dollar bill.

Liz winced. "Oops. Rubles, right? I changed money before I came, but I forgot it back at the room. So much for being the sophisticated world traveler."

He laughed and pulled her close. "I'll take care of you. Speaking of which, what are you in the mood for, lunchwise? I can offer you everything from traditional Russian cuisine to a place that serves pretty decent Tex-Mex."

"Let's go traditional," she said with a grin. "I've always liked beets."

* * *

The restaurant was small, dark and intimate. Liz liked how the wooden tables were covered with thick white cloths and how the oversize chairs seemed to swallow her up.

She and David were seated by a window with a view of the street. Sunlight danced on the polished wood floors.

"Everything is good here," David said as he handed her a menu.

She glanced down at the laminated cardboard, then laughed. "It's all in Russian."

"You did say traditional."

"Then you're going to have to translate."

"Fair enough. What are you in the mood for?"

They sat close to each other, their knees touching, their arms bumping. This afternoon was thousands of miles and nearly five years from their last lunch, but there were still similarities: the need to discover everything about him all at once. The sense of there not being enough time. The wanting that lurked just below the surface.

"Liz?"

"Hmm? Oh, lunch. Why don't you decide for me?"

He placed their order, then smiled at her. "Nervous about tomorrow?"

"A little. I know Natasha is too young to remember me from my first visit. I just hope I don't scare her. I'll get to spend some time with her, but she won't be returning to my hotel with me for a couple of days."

"You'll both need to adjust."

"Me more than her." She bit her lower lip. "I want to be a good mother."

"Why would you doubt yourself?"

"Lack of experience."

"So you'll learn as you go. Isn't that what usually happens?"

"I guess."

What she didn't say is that many new mothers had assistance from family members. There were other women around who knew what the different cries meant and what to worry about and what was no big deal.

"How old is she?" he asked.

"Four months."

"Can she do anything? Walk? Talk?"

Liz laughed. "She's just learning her multiplication tables, but we're going to have to wait another week until she masters fractions."

He grinned. "Is that your way of telling me no?"

"Pretty much."

"I'm not a baby person. I don't know from timetables."

"She can hold up her head and will soon be rolling over."

He leaned closer. "Sounds exciting."

A wild and potentially insane idea popped into Liz's head. She tried to let it go and when she couldn't, she opened her mouth and blurted it out.

"Would you like to come with me tomorrow when I go see Natasha at the orphanage?"

Three

Liz shifted impatiently in the passenger seat of the station wagon. Beside her, Maggie Sullivan navigated the route from the hotel to the orphanage.

"Nervous?" the Portland-based social worker asked cheerfully.

"You bet."

"There's no need to be. All that's going to happen today is that you'll get a chance to spend some time with Natasha. If the connection is still there and you want to adopt her, then we'll move forward with the process. If not, you're free to leave."

Liz stared at the other woman. "Does anyone ever do that?"

The pretty blonde smiled. "Not usually."

"I'm ready to bring Natasha home."

"Then we'll make that happen."

Liz hoped so. The foreign adoption process had been long enough to give her plenty of time to be sure of what she was doing. Her only concern lay in being good enough.

Behind her, the couple in the back seat talked quietly to each other. She'd met the Winstons last night at the hotel. Maggie had arranged a private dinner for the prospective parents to all get to know each other. There were eight couples and Liz. As the only single parent, she had found herself feeling slightly out of place.

Too many people going two-by-two, she thought humorously. Once again she found herself swimming against the tide. Of course this time, should she reach the distant shore, she would find David waiting for her at the orphanage.

She smiled as she remembered how shocked he'd been the previous afternoon when she'd asked him to join her. She'd been just as startled when he'd accepted. Did he have any actual interest in Natasha or was he just being polite? Liz wasn't sure she cared. At this point she would take any moral support she could get, even that reluctantly given. Besides, it wasn't as if spending time with David was a hardship. Just being in the same room with him was enough to get her hormones dancing and prancing.

They pulled up in front of the orphanage. Liz recognized the three-story gray stone building from her previous visit. This time the skies were clear and there wasn't any snow on the ground. A few flowers clung to the bushes by the front door and there was a large garden around back.

But Liz didn't care about the foliage or even the weather. Her concern and apprehension faded as anticipation took its place. After five weeks, she was going to see Natasha again. How much had the baby changed and grown? Would it take long for them to bond?

She bounded out of the car and hurried up the steps. The Winstons were right behind her, trailed by Maggie.

Liz pushed open the front door and stepped into the large foyer. Several people stood in front of the main desk, but Liz's eyes were drawn to the right, to the man leaning against a wall. When he saw her, David straightened and approached.

Her heart gave a little shimmy. Already breathless with anticipation at the thought of seeing her baby, Liz found herself even more light-headed at the sight of him. Apparently her body really couldn't take too much excitement.

He walked up, smiled and kissed her cheek.

"Your eyes are glowing," he told her. "Somehow I don't think that's all from seeing me."

Man, did he look good. A dark suit, pale yellow shirt and a tie. The combination of success and power made her mouth water.

"Some of it is about you," she said. "Some is about the baby."

"If I have to come in second, I'll accept the position if it's in relationship to your daughter."

Maggie walked up and joined them. Liz introduced the social worker to David.

"You're part of the Logan family, aren't you?" Maggie asked as she shook David's hand. "I escorted your parents on their last trip to Russia. They're both wonderful people."

"Thank you," David said.

"Miss Duncan?"

Liz turned toward the voice and saw a teenager hovering in the hallway. Slight, with long dark hair and big eyes, she was pretty, if too thin. Liz searched her memory for the name, then smiled.

"Sophia?"

The teenager nodded shyly, then ducked her head. "Yes. Hello."

Her English was stiff and heavily accented, but amazingly clear. As Liz's Russian consisted of *da* and *nyet* she wasn't in a position to complain.

"You're still here," she said as she approached the girl, leaving David in Maggie's well-manicured clutches. "I wasn't sure you would be."

Sophia shrugged. "I like to work with babies. They let me."

"You're an amazing volunteer."

Liz had met Sophia on her last visit. The teenager showed up every day to help out with the babies. Liz hadn't been able to learn much about her family. Maggie said the staff suspected she was an orphan herself and made her welcome. No one knew where she went each night or how she supported herself, but she was brilliant with the children and the orphanage needed all the help it could get.

"How is Natasha?" Liz asked.

"Good. Big." Sophia smiled. "She makes noise."

Liz's heart clenched. "Like she's trying to talk?"

The teenager nodded. "Many children were sick, but not Natasha. She is strong. She—"

Sophia caught sight of David approaching and froze. Liz quickly introduced the two, mentioning that David worked at the United States embassy.

Sophia relaxed a little when he greeted her in Russian. Liz sighed. If she'd known she would one day adopt a Russian baby, she would have paid more attention when her nana had tried to teach her the language.

"Ready?" Maggie asked.

Liz nodded and the social worker led her toward the nursery.

The babies were kept on the second floor. Cribs filled three large rooms with big windows that let sunlight rain onto the scarred but clean hardwood floors. Stacks of diapers and other supplies lined the walls. In the cribs some babies were sleeping, while others cried. On the other side of the hallway were the playrooms where the staff and volunteers interacted with the babies, a few at a time. But there was never enough staff or resources.

Liz followed Maggie into the middle room, then down the center aisle to the last crib on the right. Liz's heart beat faster and faster until she wondered if it would simply take flight. She couldn't breathe, couldn't think, not when she saw a dark-haired baby happily staring up at a brightly colored mobile made up of carousel horses.

"Natasha," she whispered as she stepped next to the crib and dropped her purse on the floor.

She smiled down at the big eyes, the chubby cheeks and perfectly shaped mouth.

"How's my girl? How's my very best little angel?"

Moving slowly so as not to startle the baby, she picked up Natasha and held her close. Her scent was as familiar as her face. Yes, she'd grown, but Liz would have recognized her anywhere.

"Natasha, I'm back. I told you I'd come back and here I am."

She knew the baby couldn't possibly understand or remember her, but Natasha didn't squirm or complain. Instead she relaxed into Liz's arms, as if sensing everything was going to be all right.

Liz heard footsteps. She turned and saw David and Sophia walking toward her. The teenager's expression tightened slightly, as if she were uncomfortable.

Probably all this western emotion, Liz thought humorously. Strangers hugging babies as if their lives depended on the moment. No doubt the teenager thought they were odd.

"You've done wonderfully well with her," Liz told her.

Sophia nodded, then slipped out of the room. David moved closer.

"So this is the lucky little girl who gets to go home with you," he said lightly. "She's a beauty."

"I know. And she's really smart."

He grinned. "You can tell that how?"

"Instinct."

Liz laughed as she spoke. David glanced from her to the baby she held. He didn't know much about kids, and this one pretty much looked like all the others he'd seen. What made her special was the love in Liz's eyes.

He hadn't been able to figure out the adoption angle. Liz was young, healthy—why wouldn't she have a baby of her own? But now that he saw her with the infant, he knew she was already a goner. Whatever her reasons for coming here, she'd made the decision to fall for Natasha.

Was that what happened with an adoption? Did the parents make a conscious decision to open their hearts to the children? He'd never considered the relationship in those terms—that it was love by choice. Is that what had happened with the Logans when they had adopted him and his sister?

"I'm shaking," Liz said, then grinned. "I know, I know. You think I'm crazy."

"No. I think Natasha is a very lucky little girl. You love her with your whole heart. I can tell."

"Really?" Liz beamed at him. "I do. I just hope she knows it, too. Doesn't she look great? They've really taken care of her."

"Sophia was telling me that she spends her volunteer time with three different babies, including Natasha."

"I know. She's amazing. Maggie told me when I was here before that Sophia is one of their best volunteers. She showed up three months ago and started helping."

Liz tucked Natasha closer and tickled her tummy. "How's my best girl? Can you laugh for me?"

Natasha gave a little squeal and kicked her feet.

David glanced at his watch. "I need to head back to my office."

Liz returned her attention to him. "Thank you so

much for stopping by. I know it was weird and a lot to ask, but I'm really grateful."

"Not a problem. I'm glad I had the chance to meet her." He touched the baby's bare foot. "When do you get official custody?"

"I'll be allowed to take her back and forth to the hotel with me starting tomorrow. All the legal stuff happens after that."

"So you'll be missing her tonight."

"Probably."

"How about a distraction? We could have dinner."

Liz sighed. "I would love to but I can't promise that I'll be perfect company. I may be a little on edge about the adoption. Is that okay?"

Since thoughts of her had kept him up most of the previous night, he didn't see the problem.

"Sure. Maybe I can take your mind off things."

He'd meant the statement casually, thinking more of conversation than bed, but at his words her eyes widened and her cheeks flushed.

Instantly heat cranked up in his body. Blood flowed fast and south.

She cleared her throat. "That would, um, be terrific."

"I was going to offer to cook, but maybe we should go out." Safer for both of them to be in public, he thought.

"You cook?" She sounded surprised.

"Very well. In fact, I do a lot of things well."

Their gazes locked. Need grew until it filled the massive room and threatened to push them out of control.

David wanted her with a desperation that stunned him. Had there been even a hint of privacy and time, he would have gone to her right then.

But there wasn't either and Liz held a baby in her arms. Definitely a clue to back off.

"We should go out," he said at the same moment she told him, "I'll come to your place."

The words hung in the air.

What he *wanted* to do and what he *should* do battled within him.

He took a piece of paper out of his jacket pocket and scribbled down a phone number.

"Call me at the office," he said as he tucked the paper into her purse. "If you want to go out, I know some great places. If you want to stay in, I'll cook."

Then giving in, because he didn't have a choice, he leaned close and pressed his mouth to hers.

Their lips clung in a kiss that was both sweet and passionate. He could taste her and the promise of what could be between them. He wanted to pull her close and touch her everywhere. He wanted to push his tongue into her mouth to discover what made her moan and squirm and surrender. He wanted a lot of things.

Instead he straightened.

"Call me," he said as he brushed his fingers across the baby's cheek and smiled at the two of them.

"I will," Liz promised.

He walked out, pleased to notice that she'd been more than a little breathless when she spoke.

* * *

David arrived back at his office in time for the weekly briefing where ongoing cases were brought up to date and potential problems were discussed.

He collected the files he would need and headed for the conference room. As he walked, he pushed thoughts of Liz out of his head. No way did he want to be distracted by her, even though she was the best kind of distraction he knew.

Forty-five minutes later, most of his staff had filled him in on what was happening in Russia and the other former Soviet countries. Ainsley Johnson spoke last.

"Another child has been taken from an orphanage," she said, sounded determined but weary. "This makes fifteen in the past twelve months."

David flipped to his file on the black market baby ring. While he didn't have jurisdiction to investigate on Russian soil, the theory was that many of the babies were making their way to the States.

"They're all the same," she continued. "The babies are all healthy, too young for official adoption, and just vanish from their cribs. They're between two and eight weeks old, both boys and girls." She shook her head. "That's the end of the pattern. Different orphanages have been hit at different times. No one on the staff suddenly goes missing, no one has extra money. Outsiders are carefully screened. So who's doing it?"

David noticed she didn't ask why. There was no need; the motive was clear. Money.

He thought about Natasha and how the baby had

looked in Liz's arms. He wouldn't want anything to happen to either one of them.

"None of the babies taken were up for adoption?" he asked.

Ainsley shook her head. "Technically they would be as they got older, but none had gotten very far in the process. No potential parents had arrived to visit, if that's what you mean."

He gave her the name of a couple of contacts. "They might know something."

"Thanks, boss."

They concluded the meeting and David headed back to his office. As he went, he wondered about the babies who had been kidnapped. Were desperate couples paying for children they couldn't get any other way?

From that thought it was a short trip to Liz-land where he quickly got lost in the memory of their brief kiss. He couldn't remember the last time he'd had it so bad. There was definite chemistry between them.

Torn between what he wanted and what he knew was the right thing to do, he briefly considered withdrawing his offer to cook. He had a feeling if she showed up at his place that night, they weren't going to get to dinner.

"This is so stupid," Liz said as she brushed the tears from her cheeks.

"You will be back tomorrow, yes?" Sophia said as they walked toward the stairs.

"I know. It's just that I'm here and I want to take her

with me. I hate the thought of her spending another night here. She's all alone."

The teenager stared at her. "You love the baby?"

Liz sniffed, then nodded. "More than I can say." Pain inside of her grew. "I keep telling myself it's just for a few more hours. Then I can take her with me and we never have to be apart."

At the front of the orphanage, Liz paused and looked up at the gray building.

"She's okay here, isn't she?" she asked desperately. "She won't think I've abandoned her?"

Sophia's big eyes remained solemn. "She will be here in the morning. Soon you take her to America and give her a good life. So many people come and take babies for a better life. Is right, yes?"

"I hope so."

Sophia offered a slight smile, then waited with Liz for the cab she'd called. Liz had thought about going back to the hotel to freshen up, but suddenly she couldn't wait to get to David's place.

She handed Sophia a piece of paper with David's address, which she got when she'd phoned him a while ago. The teenager gave it and other instructions to the cabdriver.

"The fare is set," Sophia told her. "Don't pay more."

"Thank you. I'll be back in the morning."

Sophia waved and stepped back from the cab. Liz slid onto the cracked seat and slammed the door.

Twenty minutes later Liz stepped out in front of an old, elegant building. Panes of thick glass surrounded the double-door entry. Tall, narrow windows marched across each of the five stories. Small balconies dotted the facade.

Liz paid the taxi fare, then crossed to the front door. A panel there listed occupants with a button next to each name. Only one space was blank. She pushed the buzzer and waited.

"You made it," David said, seconds later. "Come into the foyer and I'll be right down."

When the door buzzed, she stepped into the building.

The entryway was huge—open and at least three stories high. Two old-fashioned elevators stood on the left with a long wooden counter on the right. The arched ceiling was covered with blue and gold tiles.

After a couple of minutes she heard footsteps on the marble and turned to see David hurrying down the curved stairs. He crossed to her and took both her hands in his.

"You've been crying," he said. "What happened?"

She sniffed. "I tried to repair my makeup on the drive over. I guess I didn't do a very good job."

"You look beautiful and the signs are subtle. I'm trained to notice. Everything okay?"

She wasn't sure if he pulled her close or she stepped into his embrace, nor did she know if it mattered. One second he was holding her hands and the next she was in his arms.

She buried her face in his shoulder and did her best to hang on to her control. Deep breaths, she told herself, while she savored the heat of his body and the sense of safety and security that filled her.

"Liz?"

"I didn't want to leave her. I know that's completely silly. Natasha has lived in that orphanage since her mother abandoned her nearly four months ago. She'll be fine. I only have to wait until tomorrow. But I don't want to."

She felt his lips brush the top of her head.

"You're not silly in the least. You love her and you want to be with her. You're also tired from your trip, and in a strange place. All of that is bound to throw you off."

"You're being sensible," she said, holding on even tighter.

He'd discarded his suit jacket, so she could feel his firm muscles under the softness of his shirt.

"Sensible, charming and a great host. Come on upstairs and I'll show you around."

"Okay."

Reluctantly she released him. Fortunately, David looped an arm around her and pulled her against his side for the walk to the elevator. When they stepped inside, he closed the doors and pushed the button for the fifth floor. The old mechanism ground to life.

When they stepped out on the top floor, Liz had an impression of marble floors and real wood molding before she was even ushered into David's spacious apartment.

The ceilings were at least fifteen feet high. A large living room flowed into a dining area. To the left was the kitchen, to the right she caught a glimpse of a bed-room.

"Very nice," she said as she took in the blue-pat-terned sofa and the carved and inlaid tables. "You dec-orate the place yourself?"

"Don't be too impressed," he said as he dropped his arm to his side. "I rent it furnished. The view is great, I'm close to work and the price is right. I can live with it being a little fussy."

She fingered the crystal beads hanging from the base of a lamp shade. "Are you more an antler-and-gun-rack kind of guy?"

"No, but I'm not into brocade, either." He walked to-ward the kitchen. "How about a drink? Wine? Vodka?"

She set down her purse and followed him. "Wine would be great. So where did this building come from? What did it used to be?"

"Some rich guy's house about a hundred years ago. It was converted to apartments after the revolution. It's been modernized two or three times. The electrical's okay, but the plumbing makes me swear every morn-ing."

The kitchen was also large, done in green-and-cream tile with dark wood and glass cabinets. The appliances were relatively new, the countertops aging, the view to die for.

She took the glass of white wine David offered and sipped.

"Better?" he asked.

"I think it may take a couple of glasses for me to get

perky." She sighed. "I'm sorry. I'm not being very good company."

"Would you rather take a rain check?"

She looked at him, taking in his strong features—his wide, dark eyes, his firm mouth. He had a stubborn jaw and the posture of a man used to getting his way.

"I'd rather stay," she told him honestly. "Can you stand it?"

"You're not a hardship."

Suddenly tension crackled. She welcomed it not only because it was a distraction but because it was such a part of her relationship with David.

"What am I, then?" she asked.

His expression tightened. "Don't go there."

"Why not?"

"Because we both know what will happen."

She *did* know. She'd known from the first time she'd met him. Circumstances had prevented them from acting on what they'd both wanted, but that didn't change what should have been.

"What am I?" she asked again.

"A fantasy."

"I'm not sure I can live up to that."

"Want to try?"

She smiled. "Oh, yeah."

Four

Liz had enough time to think that she hadn't been with a man in forever and to worry that she'd forgotten what she was supposed to do before David moved close and took the wineglass from her hand. He set it on the counter, then cupped her face in his hands and pressed his mouth to hers.

At the first brush of his lips, she knew it didn't matter what she remembered and what she forgot. With David she would be working on instinct. Heat flared between them, passion exploded and all she could feel was a desperate need to be as naked as possible right now.

As he moved his mouth against hers, she rubbed her hands up and down his chest. His hard muscles made her want to whimper. This was a man who kept himself in terrific shape, and she had a feeling that would translate to the bedroom.

He continued to kiss her lightly, to hold her face, as if prolonging the moment. Then he slid one hand into her hair and licked her lower lip. She felt the tingles all the way down to her thighs and places in between. She parted for him, catching her breath in anticipation of his tongue stroking hers, of the way he would taste and tease and—

He plunged inside of her and fantasy became reality. She might not have seriously kissed the man in five years, but she remembered everything about their being together. Their bodies still seemed made for each other, with hers fitting perfectly against his. She moved her hands from his chest to his back so she could step right against him.

Need pulsed through her, blood rushed in her veins and her body wept with delight. She was both on fire and desperate for more of his warmth.

He released her jaw and dropped his hand to her hip, then around to her rear. When he traced the curve, she arched forward, bringing her belly in contact with his erection. Her insides clenched when she felt his arousal.

"Liz," he breathed, and began to kiss along her jaw then her neck.

Her head dropped back to give him more room. Shivers rippled through her as he nibbled on the soft skin by her ear, then licked where he'd nibbled. Her breasts ached, her nipples were impossibly hard. She was on fire and hungry.

When he put his hands on her rib cage, she caught her breath. He began to move higher, toward her breasts, and it was all she could do not to beg.

He closed over her curves. Air rushed from her lungs and her knees threatened to buckle. Things only got better when he began to lightly stroke her nipples. He returned his mouth to hers and she opened for him instantly.

They kissed deeply, the movements of their tongues matching the gentle, erotic stroking of his fingers. It was too much. It would never be enough. She wanted him in a way she'd never wanted a man before.

He raised his head. She felt the movement and opened her eyes, only to find him looking at her. Passion darkened his irises to the color of midnight. Need tightened his mouth and hollowed his cheeks. He looked like a man in serious pain.

"We're moving way too fast," he murmured.

His words were so at odds with his expression that she nearly laughed. However she had enough rational thought left to realize he was giving her a chance to pull back without having to worry about hurting his feelings.

Ever the gentleman, she thought, wondering how it all would have been different if they'd met under other circumstances and he hadn't been leaving the country five years ago.

Liz thought about her options. She'd never jumped into bed with a guy like this before. In her world, she liked things to move much more slowly. She could count her lovers on the fingers of one hand and still have room for more. Rationally, she knew she should stop this right now. It made sense. Despite the attraction, they barely knew each other.

He started to step away. Instinctively she grabbed him to hold him in place.

"Don't stop," she whispered.

Fire flared in his eyes, but he didn't move. Not even when she rubbed her belly against his hardness.

"Are you sure?" he asked, his voice low and strained.

She smiled and reached for the buttons of her long-sleeved blouse. "Absolutely."

She never got the chance to unfasten even one. Not right then. He wrapped both arms around her and pulled her even closer. His mouth claimed hers in a deep, passionate kiss that had her heart racing into hyper-drive.

His hands were everywhere. He touched her back, her arms, her shoulders, her breasts. He broke the kiss long enough to bend down and suck her right nipple through the layers of her blouse and bra. The wetness, the friction, the heat all made her cling to him.

"More," she breathed.

Then they were moving. Kissing and walking and bumping into the table, the door frame, the small cabinet in the hallway. Liz had a brief impression of space and a massive bed as they entered the bedroom, then he was pulling her blouse from her pants and working on the buttons.

This time he managed to complete the task. As he pulled off the garment, he kissed her neck, her collarbone, her shoulder, then he slipped lower and licked the valley between her breasts.

Goose bumps broke out on her skin. She reached her arms back and unfastened her bra, then straightened her arms so it fell to the floor. He groaned and lowered his head to her breasts.

The first stroke of his tongue on her bare skin had

her catching her breath. The second made her moan. When he took her tight nipple into his mouth and sucked, it was all she could do not to scream.

She clung to him, unable to do anything but lose herself in the moment. Her body swelled in anticipation and she suddenly wanted to be on the bed, with him inside of her.

Apparently he could read her mind. He pulled back and went to work on her pants.

"I can do that," she told him with a strangled laugh. "Why don't you take care of yourself?"

Less than a minute later they were both naked.

He was so beautiful, she thought as she studied the muscles in his chest, his flat stomach and his jutting arousal. She itched to draw him, to capture the moment forever. But there were more pressing needs, namely the throbbing wetness between her thighs.

They moved to the bed in synchronized movements, as if they'd done this a thousand times before. As if they'd practiced and loved until they'd gotten all the kinks worked out. She slid across the mattress while he settled next to her. She reached for him as he moved closer.

He stroked her breasts, her belly, then lower, between her thighs where she was so wet and hot, he groaned. He kissed her mouth as he explored her secrets. In less than five seconds he found that one point of pleasure and began to tease it. In less than two minutes she was tense and panting.

She could feel her release building and forced herself to open her eyes.

"Be in me," she whispered.

He raised his head and stared back at her, then nodded. After pulling a condom out of his nightstand drawer, he slipped on the protection then moved between her thighs.

She guided him inside.

He was large enough to stretch her and fill her until she gasped. In and out, over and over. They found the perfect rhythm in a matter of seconds and then both of them were breathing hard, barely holding on.

She grabbed his hips and pulled him in deeper, needing all of him, wanting the—

Her orgasm caught her off guard. One second she'd been reaching and the next she couldn't do anything but feel the endless ripples and contractions as her body surrendered. David caught his breath, then groaned. He pumped harder and faster, making her climax go on and on until he shuddered and was still.

Second thoughts took less than two minutes to intrude. As soon as David withdrew and rolled over to lie next to her, Liz had a bad feeling that she'd just made a huge mistake.

She barely knew the man and she'd gone to bed with him? What was up with that? She felt exposed, vulnerable and raw.

Telling herself she'd simply reacted to jet lag, emotional circumstances and a ghost from her past didn't help.

"You okay?" he asked.

She turned to look at him and saw the concern in his

dark eyes. Telling the truth never crossed her mind. "Sure. Great. You?"

"Fine."

An awkward silence collected. Liz sat up and glanced around. "I should probably, um, get dressed."

What she wanted to do was leave, but she wasn't sure how to say that without it coming out wrong.

She collected her clothes, then stepped into them. He pulled on boxers, then put on jeans and a sweatshirt. When they were finished, they stared at each other in the gathering twilight.

"I should go start dinner," he said.

Liz swallowed. "I'm not that hungry. It was a long day and I'm still kind of out of it from all the time changes."

He continued to stare at her but didn't speak.

She folded her arms over her chest. "I had a good time. I mean, you were great and we obviously do well in bed. It's just…"

"Too fast?" he asked.

She nodded. "Sort of. I guess we got carried away."

It was more than that. Fear lurked in the back of her mind, roaming through her thoughts like a great beast. She knew she wanted to run away because if she stayed, she risked connecting, and she didn't want that. She didn't want to fall in love. She knew what came next. Love meant death—and she had a child to live for.

"Come on," he said, grabbing her hand and pulling her into the hallway. "I'll drive you home."

They didn't speak in the car. Liz was torn between apologizing, saying it might be best if they never saw each other again and asking if he was free the next evening. She was tired, confused and still tingling from their lovemaking. Had anything ever made less sense?

When David parked in front of the hotel, she reached for the door handle. "You don't have to get out," she told him.

"Are you all right?" he asked.

She smiled slightly. "I will be."

He studied her face. "I shouldn't have pushed things."

"You didn't. I was practically begging. We were both—" She swallowed. "I guess it was just chemistry. It happens. Good night."

She stepped out of the car.

David watched her until she entered the hotel, then he pulled back onto the street. He couldn't regret what they'd done, even if he wished things had ended differently. Liz was special.

But maybe this was for the best, he thought. There was no point in continuing a relationship that was destined to end eventually. Why risk falling for her when he knew she would walk away as soon as she learned that he wasn't anything she thought he was? That he was one of the broken ones who seemed to fit in on the outside, but was never a part of the world. Falling in love wasn't an option. Not now, not ever.

Everett Baker paid for his lunch then stepped out of line and into the seating area of the Portland General Hospital cafeteria. It was close to one and most of the tables were filled with staff members or families of patients.

He saw a group of doctors by the east window, a large family next to the door, and over by the south window sat four nurses.

He told himself not to look, then found himself staring as the women laughed. Nancy Allen laughed loudest of all. Her mouth opened wide, her short brown hair swayed, and when she leaned toward one of her friends and said something he couldn't hear, the laughter erupted again.

His chest tightened at the sound. He wished that he could walk over and pull up a chair. That the women would greet him like an old friend, while Nancy gave him that special smile she had. He wanted to nestle his tray next to hers, gaze into her hazel eyes and have her tell him how much she'd missed him.

None of that was ever going to happen, he told himself. Nancy Allen didn't know he was alive.

Everett turned away and found a small empty table against the far wall. He set down his lunch tray, then pulled a paperback book out of his back pocket. He would read while he ate, the way he always did. Alone. Wanting things to be different but not knowing how to change them.

He flipped to the right page and began reading. At the same time he picked up his sandwich and took a bite. But the familiar routine didn't comfort him, nor could he concentrate when he kept hearing laughter from across the room.

He stole another look at Nancy. She was sure pretty. About his height, but slender and feminine. Sometimes, when he allowed himself to fantasize about her, he thought that they would look good together. That she was the kind of woman to make a man walk taller, prouder. With her, he knew he could feel…special.

Nancy looked up and caught his gaze. Everett turned away and quickly focused on his book. He didn't want her to know that he liked her, thought of her. He didn't want her feeling sorry for him.

He tried to bury himself in his book, but the words all blurred and his sandwich tasted dry.

He wished he was different. He wished he was like the doctors he saw around the hospital, the ones who always seemed to know the right things to say to the women they met. He'd tried to come up with a few lines, but they'd all sounded stupid. Honestly, he was much better with numbers than with people. But if things were different…

"Hi."

Startled, Everett dropped his book as he looked up. Nancy Allen stood by his table.

"Uh, hi."

She smiled and indicated to the empty chair across from his. "May I?"

"Um, sure."

She sat down and looked at him. "Do you work at the hospital or at Children's Connection next door? I've seen you around here."

He stared at her, at the way her hazel eyes were bright with humor, at her full mouth and the way it curved, at the shine of her hair as she moved her head. God, she was so beautiful. Perfect. And she'd just asked him a question.

"Wh-what?"

She smiled and leaned close. "Okay, so here's the thing. You're supposed to tell me that you've noticed me, too, or I'm going to feel really stupid."

"Oh. Sorry. Sure. Of course I've noticed you."

Color stained her cheeks. She ducked her head, then smiled at him from under her lashes. "I'm glad. Because coming over here and talking to you has pretty much taken all the courage I have, and if you'd blown me off..."

"I would never do that. I think you're great."

Now it was his turn to be embarrassed. He couldn't believe that this was happening. That she was sitting here, talking to him.

Silence stretched between them and he desperately tried to think of something to say. Anything. He wanted to compliment her, to make her feel special, to let her know that she was the most amazing woman he'd ever met. But the words got tangled up in his throat.

She tilted her head. "We could have lunch together sometime."

Relief nearly made him giddy. Of course. Why hadn't he thought of that? "Great idea. I'd like that a lot."

"Good. We'll do that." She glanced at her watch and sighed. "I'm due back on the floor. But I'll see you soon?"

"Sure. You can bet on it."

She rose and then held out her hand. "By the way, I'm Nancy Allen. A nurse on the maternity floor."

He already knew that, but didn't admit it. He didn't

want her to think he was some creepy guy who'd been spying on her.

He stood and took her hand in his. Her skin was soft and warm and he felt a flicker of desire shoot through him.

"Everett Baker," he said. "I'm an accountant here at Children's Connection."

"A man with a head for business. I like that."

He smiled because speaking was physically impossible.

"I'll see you around, Everett," she said as she pulled her hand free and headed for the door.

He watched her go, then slowly sank back into his chair. His head spun with possibilities. Nancy had talked to him. She seemed to like him. This was turning out to be the best day ever!

Liz sat in a rocking chair and held baby Natasha close to her chest. She breathed in the scent of powder and baby skin and did her best to get lost in the moment. Staring into the infant's big, blue eyes relaxed her and made her believe anything was possible. Even her brain had finally slowed down from nearly fifteen hours of whirling and considering and worrying.

She shouldn't have slept with David. Not that she was sorry; the experience had been amazing. But things had gotten weird afterward and she'd wanted to duck out and he'd let her and when she'd gotten back to her hotel room she'd started to miss him and regret bolting at the first sign of fear, but what else was she supposed to do when—

Stop!

She gave herself the command as forcefully as she could, then had to smile. So much for her brain slowing down. Between wanting to see David again, knowing it was best that she didn't, and worrying about Natasha, she'd barely slept.

"But I'm here with you now," she told her soon-to-be daughter. "And that's the best part of my world."

Sophia walked into the nursery. The teen wore her dark hair pulled back, and there were shadows under her eyes as if she, too, hadn't been sleeping.

"Morning," Liz said with a smile. "Are you all right?"

"Fine." She touched the little girl's cheek. "She remembers you from yesterday."

"I hope so. She's awake, but quiet."

"She is a good baby. Some cry all the day, but not her."

"They told me you've spent a lot of time with her," Liz said.

"Her and others. I like to be with the babies." Sophia's mouth tightened.

From what? Liz didn't know what she was thinking, nor was she sure she should ask. "Sophia, how old are you?"

"Seventeen."

She looked younger. "Do you have family around here?"

"No. In the country. A long train ride away." She touched the blanket around the baby. "She likes to be held after she eats and she likes being in the sun. She likes singing."

"You've been very good to her." Liz grimaced. "You're going to miss her."

Sophia shrugged. "There are many babies in Moscow. Babies with no family. Others will come to take her place. They will be alone and sad. Last month twins were here. They left for America. Natasha will have a better life there, yes?"

"Yes."

Liz was determined to make that happen.

"Then it is all right."

The teenager smiled and turned away, but not before Liz saw the tears in her eyes. Her heart tightened in empathy. How horrible to bond with these babies and then watch them be taken away by someone else. Was the promise of a better life enough?

Liz couldn't help thinking about Sophia. Where she lived and what she did when she wasn't helping at the orphanage. Did she really have a family as she said, or was the young girl completely alone?

Liz spent much of the day with Natasha. While the baby slept, she attended a workshop run by Maggie Sullivan. The social worker explained the rest of the adoption process and what Liz and the other adoptive parents could expect for the remainder of their stay in Moscow.

Shortly after four, Liz collected the baby's few belongings and tucked them into a diaper bag. This was it. Her first night as a parent. She settled the bag over her shoulder, then picked up Natasha and headed for the stairs.

Two other sets of parents stood there with their babies. Liz glanced around for Sophia, but the teenager had disappeared after lunch and hadn't returned.

One of the babies started to cry. The husband patted its back. The wife glanced at Liz.

"This is really it," the woman said, looking both excited and scared. "I don't know if I should do the happy dance or throw up."

"I'm thinking of both," Liz admitted.

"Sounds like a plan!"

Two cars pulled up to the curb. As Liz waited to get into the second station wagon for the drive back to the hotel, she looked at the other parents. None of the women with babies in their arms was a single mother like her.

"It's just you and me, kid," she whispered to Natasha, who blinked at her. "We'll be fine."

She didn't actually believe the words, but she felt better for saying them. On the short ride to the hotel, she tried to convince herself that everything would be fine.

Once they arrived, she had to unfasten the car seat. Maggie had put it in and now Liz had to deal with the confusing buckles. Natasha began to whimper, then cry. Liz wasn't sure if the baby was complaining about the wait or wet or hungry. Suddenly she couldn't remember the last time she'd fed Natasha. Had it been at two or at four?

The information was in the diaper bag, but that wasn't good enough. As she struggled to lift both car seat and baby from the vehicle while holding on to her purse and the diaper bag, the doubts set in. Natasha's cries increased in both intensity and volume.

"Hush," Liz said as she staggered toward the hotel. "It's okay, honey. You're okay. I'm right here."

The news didn't seem to impress the baby who only cried more.

Her purse started to slip, the diaper bag dropped off her shoulder and hit her forearm with a bone-crushing thud. She couldn't do everything and open the hotel door at the same time. This was impossible. All of it. She'd been in charge of Natasha for less than thirty minutes and she was already a failure.

Just then the door opened and someone reached for the car seat.

"Looks like you need a couple of extra hands."

Her heart froze in her chest, her mouth dropped open and she stared unbelievingly into David Logan's handsome, smiling face.

Five

"What are you doing here?" Liz asked, as surprised as she was delighted.

"You'd told me you were bringing Natasha back to the hotel and I thought you might like some moral support." He held the car seat in one hand and kept the door open with another. "Apparently you just need a pack animal."

She stepped into the hotel foyer and told herself that the need to blink compulsively was because something was in her eye—not because of emotion—but she knew she was lying. Sure, men could be thoughtful, but no one had ever done anything so wonderful as to show up just when she needed him most. Especially after what had happened the previous night.

"But we…" she began, then glanced around, aware of the other couples with their children.

Maggie walked toward her. "You came in the second car. Did everything go all right?" She smiled. "It must have. You're here."

"Barely," Liz admitted. "I'm already frazzled."

"You'll be fine. You have my room number in case you have questions or need moral support."

Liz nodded. "If all the parents have your room number, you're not going to get a lot of sleep."

"An occupational hazard." Maggie glanced at David. "You seem to have things covered."

David grinned. "I'm here to offer muscle, not baby support. I barely know which end to change."

"Liz," Maggie said with a laugh, "the man needs a quick course in the basics."

Liz figured she did, as well, but instead of saying that, she thanked the social worker and headed to the elevator.

"If you don't mind being my pack animal for just a little longer," she said, motioning to the car seat.

"Not at all. She's cute."

Liz glanced at Natasha. The baby had quieted and now stared all around. Her big blue eyes widened when they stepped into the elevator.

They rode up to Liz's floor, then David followed her to her room. Liz used the old-fashioned key, then swung the door open, motioning for him to enter.

The room was bright and large, with big south-facing windows and a small alcove perfect for the crib that had been placed there. Stacks of diapers sat on the desk, along with baby wipes and cans of formula. A single hot plate and a pot gave her a place to heat bottles.

"You came prepared," David said as he carefully set the car seat in a chair in the corner.

Liz set down her purse and the diaper bag. "I can't

take credit for the crib or the hot plate. Children's Connection provides those to adoptive parents. They also gave me diapers and the formula. It's what she's been used to eating, so her stomach won't get upset. I have some stuff I brought from the States. I'll mix in a little each time I feed her so she gets used to it gradually. Oh, and there's also baby food. Europeans generally start babies on solids sooner than we do. Of course, in France, six-year-olds have wine with dinner, so there are a lot of cultural differences that—" She shrugged off her sweater and sighed. "I'm babbling."

"You're nervous."

She nodded, then raised her gaze to his face. "I can't help it. Last night was great but weird. I don't usually—"

"Me, either," he said, stepping close and putting his hands on her upper arms. "It happened and then we both had second thoughts."

"Hence the bolting," she murmured. "Talk about not exactly mature."

"I'm okay with what we did and how we reacted. Can you be?"

She could, mostly because she liked the feel of his fingers on her arm, and how close he was standing. She liked the heat they generated, even now, and the way he smiled at her.

She nodded.

"Good." He gave her a smile. "I thought I'd stay for a while and offer moral support. Just as a friend," he added, holding up both hands in a gesture of surrender. "This isn't a subtle attempt to get you back into bed."

She was two parts relieved and one part disappointed. "If it was, it wouldn't be considered subtle." She glanced at the baby and sighed. "I would love some moral support. I'm terrified. Having an official of the U.S. government around will make me feel a lot better."

"I'd better stay in an unofficial capacity."

"Why?"

"Less paperwork."

Liz laughed. David joined in. Then he was holding her and she rested her head against his shoulder as she relaxed into him.

"You'll be fine," he murmured, stroking her back.

"Is that a promise?"

"Sure. You're motivated enough to get through the adoption process. You're intelligent, caring and determined. Why wouldn't you make a good life with Natasha?"

"Gee, when you put it like that, I'm tempted to believe you."

"You should. I'm telling the truth."

Natasha began fussing in her car seat. Liz stepped back from David and hurried to release her.

"How's my girl?" she asked as she cuddled her close.

The baby stared up at her, opened her mouth and began to cry.

"Not a good sign," Liz said. "I wonder if she's hungry."

"When did you feed her last?"

"Two," she said, suddenly remembering. Okay, maybe she wasn't a complete maternal failure. "She's going to be hungry. I need to prepare a bottle."

"You keep holding her and I'll take care of the bottle."

Liz stared at him. "You can do that?"

"If you talk me through it."

She explained what to do and watched as he performed the steps. While the bottle heated, he sat next to her on the bed and stroked the baby's cheek.

While Liz appreciated the company, she couldn't help wondering why he bothered. Having an infant around didn't exactly make the situation romantic. This wasn't his child, she wasn't his girlfriend, and yet David showed no signs of wanting to be anywhere else.

"I take it there's no significant person in your life right now," she said as he rose to test the temperature of the formula.

He glanced at her over his shoulder. "Last night wouldn't have happened if I'd been seeing anyone else."

"Oh." Right. Good point. "But the baby thing doesn't scare you?"

He grinned. "It would if you left the two of us alone. In fact, I would pass on scared and go right to panic."

"A big strong guy like you?"

"In a heartbeat." He moved the car seat to the bed and motioned to the now empty chair. "Have a seat."

She got comfortable, settled the still unhappy Natasha in her arms and offered her the bottle. The baby's mouth clamped over the nipple immediately.

"They told me she was a good eater," Liz said as she

watched her daughter drink. "I have some cereal to give her later."

He glanced at the stack of diapers. "Having Children's Connection provide those must have made packing easier."

"It did. I heard horror stories of parents traveling halfway around the world to pick up a child while only being allowed to bring one suitcase. And they had to bring all the baby supplies. At least this way I had room for some clothes for Natasha and toys."

She looked at him. Having someone else around made her feel so much better than being alone, but she knew she didn't have the right to keep him with her indefinitely.

"David, you don't have to stay."

"Are you throwing me out or giving me an excuse to leave?"

"Giving you an excuse."

"And if I want to hang around?"

Her heart fluttered. "I'd be delighted."

Shortly before midnight David stretched out on the bed and pulled Liz close. They were both still dressed and lying on top of the covers—their concession to keeping things on a "friends only" basis.

Not that clothing made a damn bit of difference, he thought humorously. He wanted her just as much dressed as he had naked. Knowing how she would look and feel and taste only intensified his desire. Not that he planned to act on it. Not again.

So he settled for the weight of her head on his shoulder and the heat of her hand on his chest. He ignored the throbbing hardness between his legs and the scent of her body. With luck, she was dealing with her own desire for him, but based on how she kept getting up and checking on the sleeping baby, he figured he was the only one in pain.

"You need to sleep," he told her. "You'll be exhausted tomorrow."

"I can't. I need to make sure she's all right. Plus you're awake. Don't you have to be alert to save the world?"

"I have a staff to help me out."

She snuggled closer. "Must be nice. So tell me about your work. What do you do, really?"

He considered the question. "I take care of problems. Some are straightforward, others are more complicated. The Russians are very proud, and like most people, they don't like foreigners interfering."

She raised her head and looked at him. "You told me pretty much nothing."

"But it sounded good."

"You're one of 'the Logans.' Were you ever pressured to go into the family business?"

"Dad was hopeful," he said with a chuckle. "But computers were never my thing."

"I guess having all those brothers and sisters helped, too. Less pressure than if you'd been the only one."

"Exactly. But I am the best looking of the bunch."

"I'll bet."

She smiled, then rested her head on his shoulder again. "I'm sorry about last night. Afterward. It was awkward."

"Agreed."

He'd been torn between never letting her out of his bed and the need to run for his life.

"Neither of us expected that to happen," he said. "I really had planned to cook you dinner."

"I know. But we're sort of combustible when we're together."

Even now, although he didn't mention that to her.

"I always thought that if we'd had more time and some privacy, we would have become lovers five years ago," she said.

He nodded. In a matter of hours she'd come to matter to him more than anyone ever had.

"I wanted you to come to Moscow with me," he admitted. "Which was crazy. So I didn't ask."

"I would have come," she told him. "I offered, remember?"

He nodded. "But your life would have been different."

"Yeah. I wouldn't have had the success, but I would have had you."

"If we'd made it work."

"We would have," she said with a confidence he envied.

She spoke without knowing the truth about him. About who he was. Liz judged him based on what she'd seen so far, but if she knew about his past—about what he'd had to overcome—she would change her mind. Not that he would blame her.

"Here we are now," she said. "In a hotel room with a baby."

"Most people just want a room with a bathroom."

She chuckled. "Be serious."

"I am."

He was—about a lot of things. "Go to sleep," he whispered. "I'll watch over you and Natasha."

That he could offer. Standing guard. Keeping her safe until she left for home.

Later that night a phone rang in a small Moscow apartment. The man who answered sat in the dark, his cigarette glowing as he inhaled.

"Da," Vladimir Kosanisky said when he picked up the phone.

"We're ready."

The American whom Kosanisky knew as the Stork sounded as if he were in the next room instead of half a world away.

Kosanisky stared at his cigarette. "The money has been transferred?"

"I just did it. You'll pick up the baby?"

"Tomorrow."

"Good. The couple waiting has paid top dollar for their kid. We don't want to disappoint them."

"No, we don't want that," Kosanisky agreed. "I'll confirm the deposit in the morning, then pick up the baby. The travel arrangements are all made. She should be to you in less than twenty-four hours."

He gave the flight information. The Stork repeated it back, then hung up.

Kosanisky replaced the receiver and dragged on his

cigarette. Stolen babies were much more profitable than importing portable stereos.

The doctor patted Natasha's tummy. "She's in excellent health," he said in a thick, Russian accent. "Good responses, alert." He reached for the chart and flipped it open. "Blood work is fine. She's young enough that you'll avoid many of the developmental problems orphan children can have."

Maggie gave Liz a knowing look. The social worker had tried to calm Liz's fears about the medical exam, but Liz had still been nervous. She didn't want anything to interfere with her ability to take the baby home with her.

While the doctor signed the medical certificates, Liz dressed Natasha in her shirt and jumper. The little girl was awake and happy, giggling as Liz tickled her feet.

"You were such a good girl," Liz whispered as she pulled the baby into her arms. "See. The doctor wasn't all that scary. He said you're healthy and that's a good thing."

Maggie collected the signed certificates and ushered Liz and Natasha out into the hallway of the orphanage.

"You're the last of the parents today," Maggie said. "So far everything is progressing well for all of you. I'm so pleased."

"Are there usually problems?" Liz asked as they walked back toward the nursery.

"There can be. A difficult medical condition can slow things down. Sometimes a medical problem can facilitate an adoption, but not all prospective parents want to take on that kind of burden. Then there's all the paperwork, the court hearing, that kind of thing. But I predict smooth sailing for you and little Natasha."

Liz hoped so. She was still fighting jet lag and now she had a night of sleeplessness to add to her stress. Not that the baby had given her a second of trouble. Instead, she'd kept herself awake, worrying and checking on the child. David had stayed with her until dawn and while she'd managed to doze in his arms, she didn't feel at all rested.

Still, thinking about David and how sweet he'd been made her feel all bubbly inside. She wasn't sure why he'd bothered, but she was more grateful than she could say.

"So what's the next step?" she asked.

"Paperwork," Maggie said with a laugh. "Lots and lots of paperwork. I've been over it twice and I'll go over it again. In your case, Natasha was simply left on the steps of the orphanage. There's no letter from her parents giving her up, so we have documentation from the orphanage saying she was unconditionally abandoned."

"Is that a problem?"

"Nope. Happens all the time."

Liz squeezed Natasha's hand. "I'll never leave you," she whispered. "No matter what."

Maggie turned a corner toward the nursery. "Next up is the court hearing. While the judge has the option of making adoptive parents wait ten days to give the birth parents a last chance to claim their child, usually the waiting period is waived. Once that happens we head over to the American embassy for a short interview. Visas are then issued for the kids and we all fly home."

It sounded simple enough, Liz thought. "When do the children become U.S. citizens? Is there a waiting period?"

"Not at all. As soon as the children legally arrive in the States, they're considered citizens. Which makes things easy."

Liz kissed Natasha's cheeks. "We'll have to get you a flag for your room," she said.

"Good idea. Oh, we're here."

Maggie stepped into the nursery and held open the door for Liz.

"I'm off to put the medical certificates into your file," she said. "I'll catch up with you later."

"Thanks for everything," Liz told her.

"Just doing my job."

Liz walked to the window of the nursery and looked out. It was a beautiful June afternoon. Sunny and warm.

"Want to play outside?" she asked the baby.

Several other children were already racing around on the lawn. A few volunteers sat with the smaller children and babies.

On her way to the yard, she paused by the main desk.

"Is Sophia here?" she asked the young woman sitting there.

"No. She did not come today."

"Huh. She said she was going to see me today."

"Plans change. With the young volunteers especially."

"Okay. Thanks."

Liz stepped out into the sunlight and glanced around. When she spotted the Winstons, she headed toward them.

"How did it go?" Diana Winston asked. A plump baby boy sat on her lap. He had a teething ring in his mouth.

"Good. Natasha got a clean bill of health."

"Little Jack did, too," Diana said.

Her husband grinned at the baby. "I think he's learning his new name. Hey, Jack, how's my big boy?"

The baby gurgled.

Liz settled on the blanket and leaned Natasha up against her midsection. Funny how she'd never considered changing the baby's name. Of course her grandmother was Russian, so that helped.

"Just a few more days," Diana said with a sigh. "Everyone is being terrific, but I'm ready to go home."

"Me, too," Liz said.

Once she could take the baby with her, there was nothing to keep her in Moscow. Nothing except David.

Wishful thinking on her part, she thought. He was being kind, but that didn't mean he was interested in anything but a very short-term relationship. They had chemistry, but that wasn't enough to hold them together. Not that she wanted anything permanent, either. It was just seeing him again. She still couldn't believe it had happened.

"We're all going out to dinner tonight," Diana said.

"Maggie knows a place where we can take the kids. We'll eat out, practice being parents and have fun. What do you say?"

"Sounds like fun," Liz said, "but I'm going to pass. I didn't sleep much last night and I'm not sure I could stay awake."

"Are you sure?"

"Positive, but thanks for asking."

Liz wasn't only exhausted, she knew she wouldn't be comfortable in that particular setting. Not when all the other parents were part of a couple. Back home she knew plenty of single moms, but here people only seemed to go two-by-two.

She had a sudden thought that she could invite David, but she dismissed it as soon as it formed. He'd been more than kind, but there was no way she was going to impose on him any more.

Later that afternoon, armed with a heavy diaper bag and a sleeping baby, Liz stepped into the cab Maggie had called for her.

The trip back to the hotel was short, despite the growing traffic. When the cab stopped across the street from the hotel, Liz paid the man and stepped out onto the sidewalk. Natasha barely stirred.

"We're doing great," she whispered to her baby. "It's been nearly twenty-four hours and so far I would say we're bonding and avoiding crisis. I vote that we continue in this pattern. What do you say, sweetie?"

Natasha stirred slightly, yawned, then settled back to sleep.

Liz smiled at her and felt her whole body fill with love. Her baby, she thought happily as she checked the traffic so she could cross the street. Her very own baby. They would be—

"You are American, yes?"

Liz turned toward the speaker and found a man standing next to her. She hadn't heard him walk up.

He was tall and thin, with dark eyes and stained yellow teeth. Instinctively she took a step back from him.

"What?"

"American."

The man said something else, but she couldn't understand him. She took another step back.

The sidewalks were crowded and someone bumped into her. She turned and the man stepped closer.

"What do you want?" Liz demanded, not liking his long hair or the unwashed smell of his body. Then she realized she didn't care about what he wanted. She glanced both ways and set out across the street.

"Wait," the man said as he hurried next to her. He kept talking, but between the traffic and his accent she had no idea what he was saying.

"Leave me alone," she told him.

He said something else, but the only words she understood were "must take baby."

Fear exploded inside of her. She clutched Natasha to her chest. "What did you say?"

Instead of answering in words, he reached toward her. Toward Natasha.

Liz screamed, which set off Natasha. The baby began to cry. Even so the man made a grab for her.

Liz spun away and ran for the entrance to the hotel. She ducked around two tourists, past an old woman, and raced inside. She headed straight for the reception desk and yelled to the man standing there.

"Someone is trying to steal my baby. Help me!"

Six

David typed the last few sentences on his computer. The quarterly report on his operative inside the Moscow police had to be deliberately vague so as not to compromise the man's position or his safety. In the past three years he'd provided invaluable information to David and the State Department.

His phone buzzed.

"Yes," David said after pushing the speaker button.

"There's a call for you. A Liz Duncan. She said it's important."

David picked up the receiver and pushed the blinking light. "Liz?"

"Oh, thank God you're at the office."

She sounded breathless and panicked. He straightened in his seat.

"What's going on? Are you all right?"

"I don't know. I guess. But someone tried to take Natasha and—" A sob caught her in throat, muffling the rest of her sentence.

Take the baby? "Liz, what are you talking about? What happened?"

"There was a man. He was talking to me, but I couldn't understand him and then he grabbed Natasha." She started to cry. "David, he tried to *take* her from me. From my arms. I don't understand. You have to get me out of here. It's not safe."

He wasn't sure if she meant the hotel or the country. "Where are you right now?"

"In my hotel room."

"Stay there. I'll call down to the reception desk and make sure they watch who comes in and out. Give me ten minutes to clear things up here, then I'll be right over. Will you be all right until then?"

"I think so."

"Good. I know you're scared, but try to relax. Everything will be fine."

He doubted she believed him, but it was the best he could do under the circumstances.

"Thanks, David. I appreciate this. I couldn't get hold of Maggie and didn't know who else to call."

"That's what I'm here for. I'll see you in a little bit."

"'Bye."

He waited until she'd hung up before releasing the line. After speaking to the clerk on duty at the hotel, he quickly finished his report and sent it, then scanned the files on his desk. There wasn't anything that couldn't wait until morning. The last thing he did was to make a call to Ainsley, one of his agents.

"I want to confirm a couple of things about the black

market baby ring," he said when she answered her phone. "They never target babies who are being adopted, right?"

"No way," Ainsley told him. "I'm guessing they don't want the trouble. Usually the babies they take are too young to have started the process. Why?"

"Someone I know is adopting an infant. I think the baby's about four months old. My friend says that someone tried to grab the kid from her arms."

"I've never heard of that happening. Was it a mugging and your friend misunderstood?"

"I'm going to find out. Thanks for the information."

"No problem."

David made his way to the hotel. If Liz hadn't been attacked by someone in the black market baby business, then who had frightened her so much and why?

He checked with the clerk who claimed to not have seen anyone suspicious-looking all day, then took the stairs two at a time until he reached Liz's floor. She opened on the first knock.

"You came," she said, flinging herself at him and hanging on as if her life depended on his arrival. "I was afraid you'd decide I was crazy or overly sensitive or just a nervous traveler."

He hugged her close, enjoying the feel of her body pressing against his. Then he reminded himself this wasn't a pleasure visit and stepped back.

"What I thought is someone attacked you and now you're scared," he said as he moved into the room and shut and locked the door. "How are you doing?"

Her long auburn hair hung down her back in loose curls. It was mussed, as if she'd been pulling frantic hands through it. Her eyes were wide and frightened, her mouth trembled. She looked as if she'd been shaken up pretty badly.

Natasha lay on the bed. Several pillows boxed her in so she couldn't roll off the mattress. She giggled when she saw him and held out her pudgy arms.

"How's my best baby girl?" he asked as he picked her up and raised her high above his head. "Did you have a busy trip home?"

She giggled again as he swooped her down, then back up. Finally he set her back on the bed and handed her a yellow terry-cloth duck.

He looked at Liz. "Start at the beginning and tell me what happened. I want to know everything you remember."

She paced as she talked, folding and unfolding her arms across her chest.

"He was tall. In his thirties, maybe. Not clean. Long hair, dark eyes. He hadn't showered in ages."

She detailed the encounter, telling him what the man had said. David took her through it a second time, then a third. He made notes on the pad he always carried with him, then reviewed them with her. When she was finished, he had her sit in the room's only chair. He crouched in front of her and took her hand in his.

"First, take a deep breath," he said. "You and the baby are fine now."

She nodded. "I'm starting to feel a little better."

"That's a start. I did some checking before I came here. While there is a black market baby ring in Moscow, they target younger infants—those only a few weeks old—and they've never taken a child who was in the process of being adopted."

Liz's green eyes darkened with fear. "So what did he want with her? Was he her father?"

"Unlikely. She's been at the orphanage since she was a couple of days old. If her father wanted to claim her, all he had to do was go there and get her back. I'm guessing the guy was a small-time crook who thought he could kidnap Natasha and then hold her for ransom. You said the first thing he asked was if you were an American. Most people assume Americans who travel are rich."

Liz pressed her lips together. "Maybe."

He didn't blame her for being reluctant to believe him. He had a feeling in his gut that something was going on, but he couldn't say what. There were thousands of abandoned babies in Moscow—why this child?

He checked his watch. "I'm going to head over to the orphanage and talk to the people there."

"Maggie stays until five," Liz volunteered. "She was in a meeting before, so she's still there."

"Good. I'll speak with her, as well. Maybe there's some information in Natasha's file. Will you be all right while I'm gone?"

She nodded. "I'm okay."

She didn't look anything but scared. "I'll come back when I'm done."

"No." She released his hand. "If you find something earth-shattering, I want to know, but otherwise, I'll deal with it." She managed a shaky smile. "There's a chance I really overreacted to what happened, right? I think your rich-American angle makes a lot of sense. The other parents went out for an early dinner, but they won't be gone long. We're all on the same floor, so I feel perfectly safe here."

He stood and looked down at her. "Are you sure? I don't mind coming back."

"Natasha is the only one of us who needs a baby-sitter." She rose to her feet. "You've already done so much for me, David. I don't want you to think I'm completely inept."

"You're not."

"Then let me prove it." She kissed his cheek. "Thank you for coming over and for following up with the orphanage."

He stared into her eyes, trying to reassure himself that she would be all right by herself.

She gave him a little push toward the door. "Go. Do your spy thing. I'll talk to you tomorrow."

He nodded. "Call me if you start to worry. You have my apartment number."

"In my purse."

He nodded, then turned to leave. "I'll be in touch."

Sophia paused on the stoop of her apartment building's rear exit. It was nearly five in the afternoon and even the alley was filled with people and cars. At this time of year there were still several hours until sunset, and residents took advantage of the light to run errands and visit with friends.

Sophia didn't want to leave her apartment, but she had no choice. She'd run out of food the previous day. While she'd held out as long as she could, eventually hunger had driven her outside.

He would be looking for her. She knew that and didn't know how to stay safe. There was nowhere to go. No one to turn to.

She'd received the first message nearly a week before, telling her it was time. The rich American couple had come through with the money and now they wanted the child they'd chosen. Vladimir Kosanisky had told her to deliver Natasha to him two days ago and she hadn't.

Kosanisky didn't know she'd left Natasha at the orphanage five days after her birth. Sophia hadn't wanted to let go of her baby, but she hadn't known how else to keep her safe. When Kosanisky had insisted on pictures of the infant, Sophia had obliged. Her hope had been that little Natasha would be adopted and out of the country before her employer claimed her. But that hadn't happened.

Sophia had been shocked to find out that black market babies were taken at a younger age than those adopted through legal channels. Fortunately, the first couple interested in Natasha hadn't been able to pay Kosanisky's price. He'd gone looking for another client, leaving Natasha in the care of her mother, or so he thought.

Sophia had visited her daughter every day, caring for her, loving her, aching to be with her always. But that wasn't possible. She wanted a better life for her baby than she'd had. A chance. In America, Natasha would be cared for and educated. She would have food and shelter and no one would expect her to make her own way in the world when she was barely twelve.

Sophia glanced around at the busy alley. When she was sure she wasn't being watched, she headed for the street and the market two blocks away.

She'd done the right thing, she told herself. Kosanisky didn't know Natasha was at the orphanage, which meant the baby was safe. The rich Americans he'd found who were so willing to buy a child would have to settle for someone else's baby. Natasha was going home with Liz Duncan. The pretty American lady would be good to her. Sophia had seen them together, had seen the love in Liz's eyes. Yes, giving up her child would tear her heart from her body, but it was the right thing to—

"There!"

She heard the single word and instantly went on alert. Even as she turned to look toward the voice, she started to run.

There were two of them. Both large and determined-looking, and running after her.

Sophia reached the street and turned right. The sidewalk was crowded, forcing her to weave between shoppers and people heading home after work.

Her heart thundered in her chest as she ran as fast as

she could. Which way was best? To the next street, then into the church? Would the market provide protection? Were there only two men after her?

The last question was answered when a white van pulled up just in front of her. She had only a split second of warning before the side doors opened and three men stepped out, including Vladimir Kosanisky.

Sophia quickly changed direction, but she was no match for them. They grabbed her and dragged her into the van. She screamed for help, but no one stopped. Only a few people even turned to look. No one wanted to get involved.

The door slid shut behind her and the van slipped into traffic.

Sophia lay where they'd tossed her. She was shaken and scared. What could she tell them that was enough truth to keep them from killing her?

One man moved into the passenger seat. Another sat by the rear door. Kosanisky settled across from her on the bare floor of the van and pulled out a cigarette.

"Did you think I wouldn't know?" he asked after he'd lit it and inhaled deeply. "About the orphanage?"

Sophia swallowed. She *had* thought he wouldn't figure it out. "You never said anything."

He shrugged. "What do I care where you keep your brat as long as she's ready when I say? But she isn't, is she? You've given her to an American."

Sophia panicked. They knew about Liz? How was that possible?

Kosanisky laughed. "You underestimated me, Sophia. Very dangerous. How many times do I have to tell you that I know everything? This is my city. I own it as much as I own you."

Panic bled into fear. He *did* own her. He had for years. She did his bidding because the alternative was to find a home at the bottom of the river.

"Natasha is going to be adopted," she said defiantly, not sure where the courage came from. "I won't have her sold. Not my child."

His dark gaze dismissed her statement. "You're a whore, Sophia. No one cares about a whore."

She didn't flinch. She'd heard worse. Besides, there was truth in what he said. She made her living on her back. What else was there for her to do?

He motioned for the man in the rear of the van to move forward. The big man grabbed Sophia by the arms. She began to squirm even as Kosanisky moved nearer. He dragged on his cigarette, then held the burning end close to her arm.

"You will get the baby and bring her to me," he said, his voice low and determined.

"No."

He pressed the cigarette into her arm. She screamed and tried to twist away, but the man holding her tightened his grip.

Sophia fought to stay aware, to not give in to the pain. As Kosanisky moved the cigarette toward her cheek, she pulled back her leg, then kicked him in the groin as hard as she could. He yelped and fell over.

Startled, the man holding her let go of her arms and

shifted toward his boss. Sophia scrambled for the rear door of the van. When it unlatched, she shoved it open and dove toward the street.

She landed hard on the road and was nearly hit by a taxi. Horns honked, her body felt broken and battered. Still, she forced herself to her feet. The pain from her fall and the burn drove her on. Even as the van swerved and looked for a place to pull over, Sophia glanced around to figure out where she was. The gleaming domes of St. Basil's Cathedral beckoned her, as did the large tourist crowd. It was the perfect place to get lost.

She limped toward a large tour group and hoped she wasn't bleeding too badly.

David walked into the main office of the orphanage and found Maggie talking with the director.

"What's up?" she asked when she saw him.

"Maybe nothing. I'm not sure."

He explained what had happened to Liz. The director, a small, balding man in his fifties, frowned.

"Why would someone want one of our orphans?"

The question surprised David. "You must know there's a black market baby ring in the city."

The man dismissed the statement with a wave. "There are rumors, but I do not believe them." He picked up a folder. "If you'll excuse me, I need to talk to one of the nurses."

David watched him go, then looked at Maggie.

"I guess denial helps him sleep at night," he said, even as he made a mental note to check up on the man.

Maggie raised her eyebrows. "I agree. Why isn't he at least concerned?" She frowned. "Oh, no. Don't tell me he's a suspect."

"He hasn't been."

"For the first time in my life I'm going to pray a man I work with is either naive or a jerk. We've had a great relationship with this orphanage. I would hate to see that change."

David pulled out a wooden chair and sat. "Don't jump to conclusions. Just because he's not willing to listen to information on the black market doesn't mean he's involved in it. He's not on any of the lists."

Maggie leaned back in her chair. "You have lists?"

He shrugged. "Part of my job."

"I don't want to know what you do." She stood and walked to the row of battered filing cabinets against the far wall. "What do you think happened this afternoon with Liz and Natasha?"

"I don't know. Either she misunderstood what was happening or someone tried to take the baby." He knew what he wanted the truth to be, but wishing didn't matter a damn.

Maggie pulled open a drawer and began to flip through files. "Maybe something in Natasha's records will give us a clue. I don't think we know anything about her parents, since she was a straight abandonment case. She was dropped off a few days after birth. It happens a lot."

"If she was just left here, how can she be adopted? There's no paperwork."

Maggie closed that drawer and opened the one below it. "You've been in Russia long enough to know that there's always paperwork. After a certain number of days, forms are filed with the court. It's routine. The orphanage wants as many children adopted as possible. Babies are the easiest to find homes for."

"Where do they come from?" he asked.

"Everywhere. Most of the children left here are born to young women barely able to keep themselves alive. There are hundreds of teenage prostitutes in the city. Most of the time they terminate their pregnancies as soon as possible. Some don't realize they're pregnant until it's too late, or they can't bring themselves to have an abortion. It's a big risk for them."

"An abortion?"

"Staying pregnant. A big belly makes it hard to make a living. What's the point in trying to have a baby while you're starving to death?"

While David dealt with the seedy side of life, his contact was usually with those buying or selling weapons, information or political power. He didn't deal with pregnant teenagers trying to survive.

"I'm guessing they don't have anywhere to go," he said.

"Of course not. If the girls give birth to a healthy child, they usually can't afford to feed it. So the babies end up here, where they're given a second chance."

"Is that what happened to Natasha?"

Maggie pulled out a folder. "There's no way for us to know, but probably."

When she set the folder down on the table and flipped it open, David leaned forward to read the contents. But there was nothing inside.

Maggie sucked in a breath. "It's all gone."

David wasn't surprised. "What was here?"

"Everything. Natasha's medical records. Staff notes. The declaration that she was abandoned. Her entire file is cleaned out." She raised her head and stared at him. "This is crazy. I just put in copies of her medical certificate myself a couple of hours ago. What happened? What does this mean?"

He didn't have any answers. Why take the contents, but not the folder itself? Had it been left in case there was some kind of casual check? Would it be removed later, when the baby was taken? Was someone trying to erase any record of Natasha's existence?

He didn't like any of this.

"Someone on my staff deals with the black market baby cases. I'm going to get her involved in this. Maybe she can find out what's going on." David wrote down Ainsley Johnson's name and handed the information to Maggie. "She'll be in touch with you. I would appreciate it if you would cooperate as much as possible."

The social worker looked shaken. "Of course. Is Liz going to be all right?"

"Liz isn't the target."

Was Natasha?

He left the orphanage and headed back to the office. He didn't want to worry Liz by showing up in her room, but he wasn't about to leave her unprotected. He made a few calls and arranged for discreet security at the hotel. Then he got in touch with Ainsley.

When she came on the line, he told her about the empty folder.

"Would the black market people take her records?"

"It's possible," she said, sounding more doubtful than sure. "Usually they simply have their own false documents. Nothing about this baby fits the profile, but I'll do some asking around."

"I appreciate that."

They hung up and David sat alone in his office. Something wasn't right, but what? And how did he keep Liz and Natasha safe for the next few days until they were free to leave the country?

Liz paced the length of the hotel room. When the phone rang, she jumped for it.

"Hello?"

"It's David."

Relief replaced fear. "What's happening? Did you find anything out?"

He hesitated just long enough to make her wonder what he was holding back.

"Not much," he said. "My contacts say it's unlikely that Natasha was flagged by the black market baby ring. But until I'm sure what's going on, I'm arranging for security on your floor. That should make you feel safer."

"Are you sure it's all right to do that?"

He laughed. "Yes. Part of my job is keeping Americans safe. That means you and little Natasha."

"Technically she won't be an American until we land in the States."

"Close enough for me."

Liz couldn't believe he'd gone to all this trouble for her. "I really appreciate all of this. You're amazing."

"So are you. Now try to get some rest. I'll be by in the morning to take you to the orphanage. I don't want you going out alone for the next couple of days."

She wasn't sure about resting, but she was more than happy to wait for David. "We'll be up bright and early."

Vladimir Kosanisky kicked an empty cardboard box out of his way as he paced the length of the small warehouse.

"She's only a girl," he yelled in Russian to the three men standing in front of the worn desk. "Seventeen. Yet, she got away and you're telling me you can't find her?"

None of the men spoke. They knew better. Kosanisky glared at them. "Worse, you sent an amateur to collect the baby. What were you thinking? Now the woman is alerted. We don't know who else she might have told. Do you want the police involved?"

They hung their heads but still didn't speak.

He understood their silence, but it annoyed him. *They* annoyed him. "You are all fools."

He crossed to the men and punched the middle one in the stomach. The man gasped and clutched his gut, but he still didn't speak.

"We must get the child," Kosanisky yelled. "Our American contact is expecting her. The baby has been paid for. She matches the physical description of what the couple wants and we don't have time to get another child."

He swore long and loudly. Sophia's escape frustrated him. She'd defied him in too many ways and she would have to be punished. Then he would take her child. But first Sophia had to be found. She knew too much and he had to keep her from talking.

Seven

Dawn came early, turning the sky first light gray, then faintly pink and finally a clear blue. Liz watched the changing colors from her chair by the window in her hotel room. She'd done her best to take David's advice and get some sleep, but she'd been too on edge.

She'd expected to be nervous about being a new mother. While she'd always loved kids, she hadn't had much contact with babies. After deciding to adopt, she'd read tons of books on baby care, attended a few classes, even the counseling sessions offered by Children's Connection. She'd done her best to prepare—and still she'd not been sure about handling Natasha on her own.

But she could deal with those insecurities. She knew that in time she would relax into her role and get better at the everyday chores of feeding and changing Natasha. But the thought that someone might be trying to steal her baby was more than she could handle. It wasn't right. It wasn't fair. She wanted all the bad stuff to go away so she could get back to worrying about things like having enough diapers and making changes in the baby formula.

She stood and stretched the kinks out of her back. After checking that Natasha was still asleep in her crib, she walked into the small bathroom and showered quickly.

The baby woke while Liz was still in her robe. She fed her and changed her and then they played peeka-boo until it was time for both of them to get dressed.

"It feels like a pink day for you," Liz said. From her suitcase she pulled out a pair of pink cotton pants and a matching shirt covered with bunnies. She dug for a pair of darling pink shoes and held them up for the baby's inspection.

"What do you think?"

Natasha waved her hands and giggled.

"I knew you'd like them," Liz said with a laugh. "I'm deeply into shoes. I think it's a girl thing. We're going to have a good time shopping for them together."

Assuming they both got out of Moscow.

Liz shook off the scary thought. She and the baby were fine, and they were going to stay that way. David was looking into things. While she might think falling in love with him was dumb, she trusted him to keep her and the baby safe.

She dressed Natasha, then herself, just in time for David's arrival a few minutes later. He called from the lobby, then knocked on her door.

"Hey," he said when she let him in. "Did you sleep?"

Liz took in the broad shoulders straining his suit

jacket, the smooth-shaven jaw, the welcoming light in his dark eyes and wanted to wave the white flag of surrender. How was she supposed to resist this man when he was not only gorgeous, but nice, great in bed, terrific with her daughter and currently keeping them both safe from mysterious forces?

"I lay down some," she said with a shrug. "I'll be okay."

His gaze narrowed. "I don't like the sound of that. Nerves keep you up?"

"I kept waiting for someone to break down the hotel room door."

"So my hallway security didn't give you much peace of mind."

"It helped. I was able to doze off now and then."

"Uh-huh. Not good. You need your rest."

She appreciated his concern, but knew there wasn't anything he could do to change the situation. "I'll catch up when I get home."

"Sure. Because Natasha won't be any trouble at all."

She smiled. "You're sweet to worry."

"I'm more than sweet. I'm practical." He crossed to the bed and pulled back the covers. "Get in there right now."

"I can't."

"Of course you can. Is she fed?"

"Yes, but—"

"But nothing. Natasha and I are going to hang out together for a few hours. We'll be back at noon to take you to the orphanage."

He looked completely serious. Even as she watched, he loaded the diaper bag, then set the car seat in the chair and carried Natasha over to it.

She resisted the need to rub her eyes. "You're really going to take care of her?"

"Do you doubt my ability?"

"Not exactly."

"Which means you do."

She shrugged. "Okay. Yes. You're a guy."

He pretended to wince. "Sexist much? Well, anything you can do I can do just as well."

"At least you didn't say better."

"I'm not that stupid."

He strapped the baby into the seat. Liz noticed that Natasha seemed just as content to be with David as with her. The kid had great taste in men.

David glanced at his watch. "Okay, you've got four hours. Sleep. I'll tell the manager to hold off housekeeping until after noon."

She sank onto the edge of the mattress and allowed herself to feel her exhaustion. "You're wonderful for doing this."

"Don't I know it." He bent over and kissed her forehead. "See you soon."

Liz watched him carry out the baby. Then the door closed and she stretched out on the bed. She really should get up and change into her nightgown. Or at least remove her jeans. Everything would get wrinkled or...

Her eyes fluttered closed and she drifted off to sleep.

* * *

David walked down to his car and strapped Natasha into place.

"You're going to change my morning plans," he told the baby. "How do you feel about staff meetings?"

The infant giggled at him, then flailed her arms. He smiled back, then climbed into the driver's seat and started the engine. As he pulled out, he noticed his parking space was taken by a white van that had just rounded the corner. Lucky driver.

When he arrived at his office, his secretary took one look at Natasha and started to laugh.

"This is new," she teased. "Are babies the latest in accessory?"

"I'm helping out a friend," he said. "She's actually a good kid." He motioned to his secretary. "Mandy, this is Natasha."

"Ooh, she's a sweetie. Can I hold her?"

"Maybe. If you're good."

Mandy laughed. "So that's how you're going to do it, huh? Tempt me with the baby, but hold her just out of reach so instead of telling you that taking care of her isn't part of my job description, I'm begging for the privilege."

"Something like that," he admitted. "Is it working?"

"Pretty much," she said cheerfully.

She followed him into his office and helped him get Natasha settled. They turned a coffee table and two end tables on their sides to form an enclosed area for the baby to stretch out in. Mandy put several blankets on the floor, while David removed Natasha from her car seat. He'd packed plenty of toys in with the diapers and food.

Careful to keep the baby in view, he crossed to his desk and picked up the phone. When Ainsley answered, he asked her to stop by later that morning, then he went to work on his own assignments.

Ainsley showed up at ten-thirty.

"Nothing new," she said as she crouched by Natasha and cooed at the baby. "Is this the one?"

"Yeah. She's four months old. Too old, you said, for the black market baby ring."

"The children have all been younger," Ainsley said as she collected Natasha and carried her to the sofa where she sat down with the baby on her lap. The tall, thirty-something blonde seemed completely entranced by Natasha's smile.

"Why risk moving such young babies?" he asked.

"They're not in the adoption process yet," Ainsley told him even as she pretended to nip Natasha's little fingers. They both giggled.

Ainsley looked up at him and cleared her throat. "Sorry. She's wonderful."

"I know."

So was her mother, he thought. But while it was safe to get attached to the infant, falling for Liz was much more risky.

"We have an assortment of problems in getting information," Ainsley said. "First of all, this is an internal issue. The Moscow police don't want our help. They barely acknowledge there's a problem. They don't cooperate. All my information comes to me from other sources. Here's what I know. Rich couples who want a baby start out working within the system, just like everyone else. At some point, they're approached by someone who says he can get them a baby more quickly."

"For a price," David said.

"Exactly. They're shown photos of babies, given health histories. They make their down payment and the child is sent over. Whoever delivers the baby has all the right paperwork and has done his homework. We've yet to find a mistake in documentation."

"So the rich couple gets a baby delivered, no muss, no fuss."

"Something like that. If Natasha was one of those babies, she should have been delivered a couple of months ago."

"Maybe the deal fell through."

Ainsley nodded. "I'm sure it happens. But why not leave her in the system for a regular adoption?"

He looked at the baby. She had big blue eyes and brown hair. Her round face and happy smile made her a candidate for a baby model.

"Does she look like someone?" he asked, speaking slowly as the thoughts occurred to him. "Is it possible to get a baby to order?"

Ainsley frowned. "You mean the couple requests a certain kind of child in appearance?"

"I don't know. It's your department. Does that ever happen?"

"I suppose it could. The couple is already paying a huge amount for the baby. Why not get one special ordered?" She grimaced. "We're talking about children here, not pizza."

"I agree, but will our friends in the black market see it any differently?"

"Probably not."

David considered the possibility. "So we don't know who wants Natasha. Or if the attack was a fluke or not. But if it wasn't, the ring could be after her specifically and not just any child. Can we confirm any of this?"

"I'll have to ask around."

"Do that and get back to me."

"What are you going to do?"

He sighed. "Figure out how to keep Natasha and her adoptive mother safe without making either of them panic." More security at the hotel for one thing, he thought.

"We could be wrong about all of this," Ainsley reminded him. "Maybe it was just a freak thing."

"Maybe, but until I'm sure, I want to take every precaution."

"You don't have to cart me around everywhere," Liz said when David stopped his car in front of the orphanage.

"You're not going anywhere alone until this is figured out," he reminded her. "No arguments. I'll be by around five to take you back to the hotel."

He turned to her. "I mean it, Liz. You're required to

check in at the orphanage, but don't go anywhere else without me. Don't go sight-seeing or even to the corner market."

He looked so stern and concerned that her heart did a little shimmy dance.

"I don't think there is a corner store," she teased.

"I'm serious."

"I am, too. Really. I'm just trying to lighten things up to keep myself from going over the edge."

"How's that working for you?" he asked.

"Can I get back to you?"

He smiled. "Sure."

They stared at each other. It was one of those moments where time seemed to stop and the world became a better, brighter place. She wanted to lean toward him and kiss him. She wanted him to kiss her back and touch her and maybe invite himself over for the night.

"I have to get back to the office," he said quietly. "I'll pick you up at five."

"I'm sure Maggie could drive me back to the hotel."

"I'm sure she could, too, but I want to do it. We'll stop somewhere and get a quick dinner."

Quick, huh? She wasn't sure she liked the sound of that. "Do you have plans for the evening?"

"Unfortunately, yes. A meeting at the embassy."

The melty feelings froze in place. Her mouth got dry and her throat tightened. "Is that a euphemism for another woman?" she asked, trying to sound interested rather than poised for heartbreak.

He leaned forward and brushed his mouth against

hers. She enjoyed the brief contact while trying desperately not to go up in flames.

"It means exactly what I said. That I have a meeting."

She could believe him or not, she told herself, and David had no reason to lie. Besides, they were hardly a couple.

"I'll be ready at five," she promised, and climbed out of the car.

He helped her with Natasha and escorted them both inside. After waving goodbye, he left. Liz headed for the nursery.

She settled Natasha for a nap, then went looking for Sophia. She hadn't seen the teenager the previous day, which was odd. On Liz's last visit to Moscow, the teenager had been with Natasha every day.

But instead of Sophia, she ran into Maggie.

"How are things going?" the social worker asked. "Are you feeling all right?"

"I'm good," Liz told her, then shrugged. "I was terrified when that man tried to take Natasha, but I'm starting to wonder if I made a fuss over nothing."

"Someone stealing your baby isn't nothing."

There was something in Maggie's gaze that alerted Liz. "What's happened?" she asked. More to the point, what hadn't David wanted her to know?

Maggie led her back into the nursery, looked around as if checking to make sure they were alone, then spoke in a low voice.

"Did David mention anything about Natasha's files?"

"No." Liz's stomach tightened. "What about them?"

"They're gone. Everything. The folder is completely empty."

Liz pressed her hand against the wall and fought not to throw up. "They can't be. We need that paperwork to get her out of the country. How can I adopt her if there's no documentation?"

"Hey, it's okay." Maggie touched her arm. "I'm sorry, I didn't mean to upset you. As far as the adoption goes, I have all the paperwork I need with me. I keep all the babies' files in a lockbox in my hotel room. We're fine. I checked everything this morning. With the medical certificate we got yesterday, you and little Natasha are good to go. We just have the court hearing to deal with. That's tomorrow afternoon. Once you're cleared through the courts, I'll take you to the embassy, you'll get Natasha's visa and then you can head home. In less than forty-eight hours you'll leave all this behind."

Liz tried to relax. Maggie was right. It was only two days. She could survive that.

"I'm thrilled you kept copies of everything," she said earnestly. "If you hadn't…"

"Part of my job," Maggie said with a shrug. "I learned that one early. So we're fine."

Liz was grateful for her efficiency. "This is making me crazy," she admitted. "I want to relax. I do for a second, then I start to think. If someone took Natasha's paperwork, then someone tried to steal her from me, the two events could be linked. Maybe yesterday wasn't just a random attack."

Maggie shifted uncomfortably. "You don't know that."

Liz figured she didn't know a lot of things, but it didn't take a genius to put the pieces together. No wonder David hadn't wanted her walking the streets of Moscow by herself.

"Why *my* baby?" she asked.

"I don't know," Maggie admitted. "Are you all right? Do you want me to take you back there?"

"I'd rather stay here," Liz told her. "David's coming by to pick me up at five. He'll take me to the hotel."

Maggie relaxed. "I don't blame you. Given the choice between being escorted by me and being escorted by him, he would win hands down any day."

Liz managed a smile. "He's very nice."

"You left out sexy."

"Okay, that, too."

Maggie raised her eyebrows. "Anything between the two of you?"

Liz didn't know how to answer that question. "I met him five years ago, just before he took the assignment in Moscow."

"Ah, so you have a history."

"Nothing that exciting. We were…friends."

Did that describe their afternoon and evening together? How would she describe what they had now? It was all confusing.

"He seems to care a lot about you," Maggie said.

"Some of that is his job."

"But not all of it?"

Liz didn't have an answer for that. She decided to change the subject. "Have you seen Sophia?"

"No. She hasn't been around much the past couple of days."

"I know and that worries me. She was here every day on my last visit. She really cares about the babies. I can't believe she'd leave them for so long."

Maggie didn't seem concerned. "The girls who volunteer aren't big on commitments. They show up for a while and then they get distracted."

"Maybe," Liz said, although it didn't sound right to her.

Liz waited until David walked her to her hotel room before mentioning Sophia to him.

"I can't help thinking that something's wrong," she told him. "Okay, maybe I don't really know her, but this doesn't seem right."

"Do you have a last name?" he asked as he set the car seat on the chair.

"No."

"I'm sure I can get it from the orphanage. Maybe send someone over to check out her apartment."

Liz stared at him. "You'd really do that?"

"Sure. We don't know what's going on with any of this. If someone from the orphanage is missing, I want to know."

She considered what she'd learned from Maggie. "Speaking of which, you didn't tell me that Natasha's paperwork was gone."

His mouth twisted. "I didn't want to upset you."

"Which makes sense, but we're talking about my child. I need to know what to look for," she told him. "If there are hidden dangers, I want to stay alert."

He nodded. "I wish I knew more. Right now I'm fighting shadows and it's damn frustrating. I haven't learned anything new. None of my contacts knows anything."

"You have contacts?"

He managed a smile. "I'm a very useful guy."

"Yes, you are."

They stared at each other. Suddenly tension crackled and Liz was intensely aware of the bed in the room. She wanted to move close to him and have him pull her into his arms. She wanted him to kiss her and touch her and take her to a place where nothing mattered but the two of them.

Natasha gurgled, as if reminding her there were three people in the room.

He cupped Liz's face. "Are you going to be all right tonight?"

"Sure. There's a burly guard down the hall, right?"

"Uh-huh. He'll stay on duty until I get back. I'll be late."

His fingers felt warm and smooth against her skin. She wanted to turn her head and kiss his palm. Instead she sighed.

"That's right. The hot date you're pretending is a big, important meeting."

"It *is* a meeting."

"So you say."

His dark eyes brightened with amusement. "Are you calling me a liar?"

"I'm saying you keep things from me."

"Only about work. Not about women." His expression turned serious. "Do you believe me?"

He was closer than he had been. She could feel the heat of him, and her body responded by melting. His free hand settled on her waist and her arms wrapped around his neck.

"I believe you," she whispered just before his mouth settled on hers.

Their kiss was everything she remembered. Deep, erotic, passionate. Her lips parted instantly, and when he swept inside her mouth, she moaned with need and pleasure.

At the first stroke of his tongue, she felt her breasts swell. At the second, her thighs began to tremble. By the third, she was close to begging.

He dropped his hands to her hips, then around to her fanny, where he cupped the curves as he pulled her hard against him. She felt his arousal. He was hard; she was wet. There seemed only one solution. Except...

He straightened. "I have a meeting," he murmured.

"I know." He had a meeting, she had a life and they shouldn't consider making love again. Not when everything was so uncertain.

"I don't usually do this," she told him. "Get involved so quickly. We're not even dating."

He smiled. "Do you want me to ask you out?"

Liz realized she did. She wanted to see David more, and not just because her life was in danger. She wanted them to spend time together, to laugh and get to know each other. But his world was here and she was leaving in two days.

"I'm not sure we're going to have time," she admitted.

"Too bad." He kissed her lightly. "I want to come back here after my meeting and check on you. It'll probably be around midnight. Is that too late?"

Check on her, huh? She wanted to read more into the statement, but had a feeling he meant exactly what he said. Business only.

"Don't worry about waking me up," she told him. "I doubt I'll sleep."

"I know. That's why I'm coming back."

He glanced at the bed, as if realizing what could happen later.

"I'll be here in an official capacity," he said.

"Is that your way of telling me not to expect you to seduce me?"

He groaned softly. "You tempt me, Liz, you have to know that. But this is about keeping you safe."

She wanted it to be about both. Wishful thinking. "You're very sweet to worry. I won't do anything I shouldn't."

"Good." He headed for the door. "Because where you're concerned, my self-control is about zero."

She laughed as he walked out the door. When she was alone with Natasha, the good feelings faded and suddenly she wanted to cry.

"I'm fine," she told herself. "We're both fine."

If only she could believe it.

Vladimir Kosanisky swore as he dialed the phone. It was picked up on the second ring.

"We still haven't found the girl," he told the American, his voice tight with frustration. "We've wasted a whole day. I say we forget about her and go after the baby."

"And if the girl talks?" the Stork asked.

Kosanisky considered the problem. Sophia had always been difficult. Too bad he'd had a soft spot for her for so long. His feelings had clouded his judgment. "We eliminate her."

"All right. When will you get the baby?"

"Tonight," Kosanisky said. "My men will break into the woman's hotel room and take it."

"Will you make it look like a robbery?"

"There's no need." He lit a cigarette. "My question is about the American woman. Elizabeth Duncan. Do you want me to kill her or not?"

Eight

Liz had always enjoyed the long summer days, but no more so than this evening as she paced back and forth in her hotel room. Logically she knew she should be safe where she was, but she didn't *feel* safe. Still, while the sky remained light, she sensed no one would come for Natasha. When darkness fell, that was another matter.

"It's all right," she told herself over and over. She would be fine. David had promised to come back and stay with her, and she trusted him completely. He would keep his word. The only question was when he would arrive.

She checked on the baby. Natasha slept soundly in her small crib. Apparently the tensions didn't affect her. Liz lingered over her, admiring the curve of her cheek and the perfect rosebud shape of her mouth.

"Pretty baby," she murmured. "Soon we'll be heading home."

Back to Portland, she thought. To her house on the river and a normal world. She'd been excited about coming to Moscow, but now she only wanted to leave.

Time crawled by and with each passing second, the sun slipped lower, toward the horizon. By nine-thirty, there was darkness in the streets and lights in the windows.

Liz stared out, her heart pounding harder and faster every time she took a breath. Her nerves were on edge, her body alert. They were going to come for her—she could feel it down to her bones. What if they came before David arrived?

"You're being ridiculous," she told herself. "There's a guard just down the hall."

David had promised her a burly protector to watch her door. Of course he could decide to take a break.

Fear swirled up inside of her, coiling low in her belly and chilling her blood. She stepped back from the window and carefully closed the blinds, then she glanced around the room, as if looking for a place for them to hide.

"We can't stay here," she murmured into the silence. Yes, David was going to come for her, but what if he didn't arrive in time? What if they got here first?

She opened her door and looked down the long hallway. Her body stiffened when she didn't see anyone. She checked both directions. Nothing.

Acting quickly before she could change her mind, Liz grabbed her room key and went next door. Diana Winston answered right away.

"Liz! What's going on?"

"I need to go downstairs and talk to the desk clerk," she said, trying to sound upbeat and casual. "Natasha's asleep, but I wondered if you'd mind staying with her for a second until I get back."

Diana smiled. "Not a problem." She retreated into the room, where she spoke to her husband, then followed Liz into the hall.

Liz left her with Natasha, then hurried down the stairs. She took the last flight quietly, hugging the far railing, staying out of sight as long as possible. Her athletic shoes were silent on the worn carpeting.

As she rounded the curve in the stairs, she saw the desk clerk sitting and reading a newspaper. A quick scan of the lobby showed her that there wasn't anyone else to be seen. What had happened to the burly guard? Had he left on a break? Had David lied about leaving someone to protect her?

Her heart pounded even harder than before, and her throat tightened. What was going on?

Every instinct told her she had to protect Natasha. So she gathered her courage, walked up to the desk and smiled at the young man.

"Do you speak English?" she asked.

"English? *Da!* Good speak." He grinned.

Liz sighed silently. This was going to take longer than she wanted. She carefully explained that she would like to change her room. Was there an empty room in the hotel?

The clerk didn't understand. She had a room now. It was a good room, at least she thought that was what he said. With his accent and broken English, it was difficult to tell. Of course her Russian was fifty times worse, so she wasn't going to be critical.

She passed him two five-hundred ruble notes, which

was somewhere between thirty and thirty-five dollars, if she was doing the math right. The young man instantly reached for the registration book.

"More room. *Da*. Near." He turned his back on her and poked through the half wall of small cubbyholes containing messages and keys.

He plucked out a key and handed it to her. "By hall," he said proudly.

"Thank you. Please don't tell anyone I moved."

He frowned. "Tell?"

"If someone asks about me…" She wondered how to make it clear that she didn't want her new room number given out. "Secret? No talk?"

"Ah." He nodded vigorously. "No say new room."

"Yes. That's right. No say new room. Thank you."

She glanced around the lobby, but there was still no sign of the guard. What had happened?

She shook off the question. There was no time to worry about that. She took the key, thanked the desk clerk again and made her way up the stairs.

She was panting by the time she knocked on her door and Diana let her in.

"All taken care of?"

"Yes. Thanks." Liz watched Diana return to her own room and shut the door.

When the coast was clear, Liz walked across the hallway and went two doors down to her new room and tried the key. It turned easily and she slipped inside. The bedroom was identical to hers, done in blues instead of greens and facing the side street instead of the main road. It would suit her purposes perfectly.

She walked back to her old room and collected the few things she would need to get through the night. She didn't want to make a lot of noise by dragging too much across the hallway.

She filled the diaper bag with formula, diapers and a change of clothing for Natasha, a book, a couple of energy bars and a bottle of water for herself. She grabbed her purse and some pillows so she could secure Natasha on the large bed they would be sharing. There was no way Liz could move the crib without waking up everyone on the floor.

When all her supplies were in place, she carefully picked up the sleeping baby and carried her the few feet to the new room. Natasha never stirred.

Once everything was in place, Liz debated calling David to tell him what she'd done, but she wasn't comfortable using the phone.

"I've watched too many spy movies," she told herself, trying to find humor in the situation. "Do I really think they're monitoring my calls?"

Apparently the answer was yes because she couldn't seem to make herself pick up the receiver. Not a problem, she told herself. She would look out the peephole and when David showed up, she would let him into her new room.

She dragged the single chair in the room close to the door so she could hear footsteps, then positioned a lamp nearby to provide light. She tried losing herself in her book, but mostly she sat and listened to the sounds of the night, bracing herself for some kind of attack that she knew logically wasn't going to come.

Shortly after midnight, she heard a faint creaking of the floorboards. Expecting to see David, she stood and peered out of the peephole. Instead two men stood in front of her old door. One bent over the ancient lock.

A scream built up inside Liz's chest. She pressed her hand over her mouth to hold it inside. The fear returned, as cold and liquid as it had been before.

This isn't happening, she told herself even as she watched them open the door and enter the hotel room.

Panic swept through her. What to do? They would see right away that she wasn't there. Would they start breaking in doors to find her?

She glanced frantically around the room, looking for another way to escape, but there wasn't one. Just the window, and she was too high up to get to the street. Could she make a rope or something? Was there a—

She forced her racing mind to halt and consciously stilled her breathing. It was going to be all right, she told herself. The men had come in quietly. They weren't looking to make trouble, or be discovered. Yes, they were searching her room, but they had no idea where she'd gone. For all they knew, she'd left the hotel.

She continued to monitor the hallway. After a couple of minutes they stepped out of her room and glanced around as if looking for clues. She ducked back before realizing they couldn't see her watching them.

One of them said something to the other. She didn't

hear any words, not even the rumble of their voices. Apparently they didn't want the other guests to know they were here. Finally they closed the door and walked away, toward the elevator and stairs.

Liz waited until they were completely gone before sinking to the floor and pulling her knees to her chest. Her body shook and she had trouble catching her breath. What would have happened if she hadn't changed rooms? Would those men have Natasha now?

Liz's eyes burned. She blinked back the tears. The danger had faded for the moment, but what was going to happen next time?

Realizing she had to act, that she couldn't just wait for the next attack, she forced herself to her feet and cautiously opened her door. The hallway was still empty. Quietly she collected her sleeping baby, walked down three doors and knocked on Maggie's door.

David found parking just past the hotel. He would have been pleased with his luck if there hadn't been two police cars stationed directly in front of the building. The second he saw them, he got a bad feeling in his gut.

As he climbed out of his car, he glanced at his watch and swore. It was nearly two. His meeting had gone much later than he'd expected. Had Liz simply panicked from the waiting or had something happened?

He hurried into the lobby and found Liz sitting on a bench and holding Natasha. Maggie stood with several police officers. Her frustrated expression told him that she wasn't pleased with the way things were going.

He crossed to Liz. "What happened?" he asked.

She jumped at the sound of his voice, rose and stared at him. He read the fear in her green eyes, and the wariness.

"Two men broke into my hotel room," she told him. "They didn't know that I'd changed rooms about an hour before. When I came downstairs to do that, there wasn't any guard in the hallway."

"What?"

She glared at him. "Are you playing a game with me, David? Was this all a joke to you? Did you lie to me, telling me someone was on duty so I'd feel better?"

He wanted to grab her and shake her. "Of course not. I left an agent stationed here. I checked in with him my-self around nine."

She didn't looked convinced. "He's not here now."

David swore under his breath. "I'll be right back."

He crossed to where Maggie stood with the police. After showing his identification, he asked what had happened.

In a matter of seconds he understood Maggie's frus-tration. The officers believed the break-in was a simple robbery. That Liz's room had been a random target. They weren't interested in possible baby theft. "Amer-icans are so paranoid," they said to each other.

He listened without offering a comment of his own. Rather than argue, he asked for details. A report would be filed, but as nothing had been stolen... They shrugged, indicating there was little they could do.

"Or want to do," David muttered in English.

Maggie nodded. "I'll admit I didn't take the first attack very seriously. Having Natasha's records missing was a little odd, but when combined with what happened tonight, there's too much evidence to ignore. Something is going on."

David agreed, but what? And where the hell was the man on duty?

He left Maggie with the police and walked out into the night. There were streets on three sides of the hotel, an alley on the fourth. He stepped into the narrow alley and began searching. He came across the guard halfway down. The man had been tied up and left behind a large trash can.

David swore as he bent over him. Even as he felt for a pulse, he reached for his cell phone and hit Auto-dial.

"It's Logan," he said when the phone was answered on the first ring. "We have a problem." He gave the address of the hotel and the placement of the guard in the alley.

"It's Green," he said. "I assigned him to watch the hallway. He's been attacked."

The guard stirred.

"He's coming around. I think they knocked him out. There's no blood. All right. Five minutes."

He dropped the phone into his suit jacket pocket and went to work on the ropes around Green's ankles. The man groaned.

"Logan?"

"It's me."

"Hell, they jumped me from behind. I heard a noise

on the stairs and I went to see what it was." He moaned quietly. "Classic mistake."

"It happens."

"Yeah, and now I've got a hell of headache to remind me. Did they get the kid?"

"No. Liz and the baby are safe."

Green sat up and rubbed his wrists. "I'm sorry I screwed up."

"Don't sweat it. No harm done."

Except that Liz hadn't believed him about the guard.

He helped Green to his feet and they walked back to the main street. A few minutes later a plain black car pulled up in front of the hotel. David helped Green into the back seat, then straightened. When he turned, he saw Liz watching him from the entrance to the lobby.

The police left about twenty minutes later. They promised to look into the attempted robbery, but David doubted they would take any action. He escorted Liz and Maggie back to their rooms, seeing the social worker inside first, then returning to Liz.

She let him in, but didn't offer him a seat. He watched as she placed a sleeping Natasha on the bed and made sure she was secured by a fortress of pillows. When she'd finished, she straightened and looked at him.

Shadows darkened the skin under her eyes. She looked bone-weary and shell-shocked. He wanted to go to her and hold her tight, but her earlier accusations kept him in place.

"I wouldn't lie to you," he said.

She nodded and sank onto the edge of the bed. "I know. I'm sorry. It's just when I went outside and there wasn't a guard, I didn't know what to think."

He could see the situation from her point of view. They didn't know each other that well, so why should she trust him? Yet, he hated that she'd been afraid and hadn't believed him.

"Someone lured the guard away and beat the crap out of him," he said.

"I figured that when I saw you walking him to the car." She wrapped her arms around her chest and bit her lower lip. "So they're willing to attack people and break into rooms just to get Natasha. She must be some baby."

He crossed to her and tugged her to her feet. When she stood next to him, he wrapped his arms around her and pulled her close.

"I'm right here," he said.

"I know."

"It's okay."

"No, it's not."

Her words were muffled against his shoulder.

He didn't like the resignation in her voice, nor the truth in what she said. It wasn't okay. Until he figured out what the hell was going on, it might never be okay.

"I just have to get through to the hearing," she whispered. "I can do that, right? One more day."

One more day and then she would be gone. He knew it was for the best—that she would be safe once she was back home—but he didn't want her to go.

He moved to the chair and sat down, then pulled Liz

onto his lap. She settled gracefully and leaned against him. He stroked her long hair.

"You'll be fine," he said. "Between now and the hearing, I'll make sure you're not alone. If I can't be here, I'll arrange for someone from the embassy staff to be with you. You'll have an escort to the hearing."

A shiver rippled through her. "I appreciate all that."

"Has Maggie explained what happens at the hearing?" he asked.

She nodded. "We have to see a judge. It's the last step before we can get visas for the children. There's a ten-day waiting period, but that's always waived. So once we finish with the hearing, we go to the embassy to get the visas, then back to the hotel to pack. Our flight leaves at midnight."

One more day, he thought grimly.

"Do you want to come to my apartment tonight?" he asked.

She raised her head and looked at him. "I'd rather not move Natasha. She's slept through all of this, but I don't want to push my luck."

"Then I'll stay here."

When she glanced at the bed, he added, "In the chair."

"You won't get much sleep."

"I've survived on less."

She leaned back against him. "Do you spend a lot of your day rescuing Americans in trouble?"

"Not usually, but I'm happy to make an exception."

"I don't know what I would have done without you," she whispered.

"It's not an issue. I'm here."

He would stay with her until she left, he told himself. He wrapped his arms around her and kissed the top of her head. The wanting, always there below the surface, flared to life. He ignored it and the subtle pressure in his groin. Neither mattered. This was about keeping Liz and Natasha safe. Once they were on the plane and heading home, he would forget about her. Or at least try.

It rained the next morning and the gray weather matched Liz's mood. She hadn't slept the previous night. Worry had combined with her awareness of David in the same room. Both had kept her tossing and turning until sunrise, when David had returned to his apartment.

But it would soon be over, she thought as she finished dressing. And it would be worth it.

She turned and smiled at Natasha who lay propped up on several pillows. The baby held a terry-cloth giraffe in her pudgy hand and stared at it with delight.

When someone knocked on the door, Liz jumped, but only a little. Maggie had already been by to check on her and tell her what time they were leaving. David had phoned to let her know when to expect the agent who would escort them to the court hearing.

Liz checked the peephole, then opened her door to admit a tall, beautiful, slender blonde holding out an official-looking identification card.

"Elizabeth Duncan?" the woman said. "I'm Ainsley Johnson. I work with David Logan. I'm here to make sure your day goes smoothly."

"Thank you. Please come in."

Liz smiled and tried not to tug on the hem of her T-shirt. She felt ratty when compared with the agent's exquisitely tailored pale blue suit and matching leather sandals.

Ainsley stepped into the hotel room. "How are you feeling?"

"Tired, but all right."

"David filled me on what's been happening. I'm sorry your adoption experience has been so difficult."

"Thank you."

Liz tried not to picture David and the gorgeous blonde breakfasting on a terrace somewhere after a night spent together. Ainsley wasn't wearing a wedding ring.

Liz shook off the unwelcome thought. She knew her lack of sleep made her edgy. What did it matter if David and Ainsley were involved? Except it did matter, which made no sense.

Ainsley crossed to the bed and smiled at Natasha. "So you're what all this fuss is about. You're certainly a pretty baby. Are you ready to dazzle the judge and go home with your new mommy?"

Natasha giggled and waved, which caused her to drop her giraffe. Ainsley leaned over and picked it up.

"You're a very special girl," she cooed. "Your new mommy must be very happy." She turned to Liz. "I know all this is stressful, but it will be over soon."

Great. Ainsley was beautiful *and* nice. This was so not how Liz wanted to start her day.

"I'm just about ready," she said. "The diaper bag is

jammed with food and diapers, along with a change of clothing."

"Good. The individual hearings don't usually take too long," Ainsley told her. "I've spoken with your social worker already. Because of what's been happening we thought it best to travel as a group. Everyone will stay in the courtroom for all the hearings, then we'll caravan over to the American embassy when it's finished. Once you get your visa, you'll stay there until it's time to go to the airport."

Liz panicked. "But I haven't packed."

"Not to worry. I'll take care of it. Part of our full-service protection plan."

Liz glanced at her watch and realized there was no time to pack everything in the few minutes she had left. But she could at least pack up this temporary room. Ten minutes later, Ainsley said it was time to leave.

The other parents were waiting in the lobby and talking excitedly. They were all eager to go home and start their new lives with their children. Maggie broke them into small groups, then ushered them out to the waiting cars.

As they drove to the hearing, Ainsley pointed out the various sights of the city. For Liz, Moscow had lost much of its appeal. To her, this was the city where she'd almost lost Natasha.

Just a few more hours, she told herself. First the court hearing, then she would be at the embassy until she flew home.

"I think you'll like your new house," she told the

baby. "You have a beautiful room that gets plenty of light. I've bought you a new crib and toys and lots of pretty clothes. We'll be so happy."

And safe. Right now not being afraid seemed like an impossible dream.

The hearings were held in a large buff-colored stone building. Liz carried Natasha up the front steps. Ainsley closely followed, carrying the diaper bag and her own satchel.

Eight sets of parents held on to their children. Ainsley maneuvered Liz into the center of the group and kept her there as they moved into the large room where they would meet the judge.

The chamber could have easily fit a hundred people. The ceiling stretched up nearly twenty feet and the whole space echoed eerily as they filed toward wooden benches and took their seats.

One by one the parents were called up to meet the judge, a stern-looking man with gray hair and glasses. He looked through their paperwork, asked a few questions that were translated by the small man on his left, then signed a piece of paper. When it was finished, he said the same thing.

"The ten-day waiting period is waived. Congratulations."

Clutching their precious documents, the happy family returned to the benches.

"Elizabeth Duncan."

Liz stood and held Natasha to her chest. Maggie accompanied her up to the judge, as she had with all the other parents. She held a folder in her hand with all the duplicate copies of the paperwork.

The judge didn't look at her. Instead he flipped through the pages several times. Liz felt her stomach sink as the fear returned. She swallowed and tried to relax. Finally the gray-haired man looked at her and said something in Russian.

She froze, unable to breathe or move.

"Please state your full name."

Liz nearly fell to her knees in relief. It was the same first question he'd asked the other parents. Everything was going to be fine.

She gave her name, then the other answers. Her heartbeat slowed to something close to normal. The judged signed several documents.

He spoke again.

"You have a beautiful little girl," the translator said. "In ten days you may apply to the embassy for your visa. Between now and then you may not take the child out of the country. Next."

Liz stared at him. "What? What did he say?"

Maggie took the paperwork the translator offered her and led Liz back to the benches.

Liz couldn't believe it. "This isn't happening," she said. Her whole body went numb.

"I'm sorry," Maggie said. "Sometimes they get fussy. You shouldn't read anything into it."

Ainsley joined them. The blond agent didn't look happy. "This isn't good," she said. "I don't like it at all."

Liz stared at Maggie. "We have to be able to do something. Can't we talk to someone? I can't stay here another ten days. They'll get her for sure."

"There's nothing we can do," Maggie said. "I'm sure everything will be fine."

But she didn't look convinced, nor did Ainsley. Liz looked at the other parents—the happy parents who would be leaving that night, while she would be forced to stay behind.

She held Natasha close and squeezed her eyes shut. "I won't let them get you," she whispered to the little girl.

She meant the words with all her heart, but how was she supposed make them come true?

Nine

David stared at a detailed diagram of the port and tried to figure out how large quantities of antiaircraft guns were being shipped out of the country. His men had been over every inch of area—the loading docks, receiving, long- and short-term storage.

Trying to gather information while not being seen by dock employees or caught by the local police added to the challenge of his work. He tapped his pen on the east entrance and looked at the man sitting across from him.

"What isn't inspected?" he asked.

Brian Arlington, one of David's field agents, shrugged. "We've looked at everything bigger than a bread box. I swear, boss."

David picked up a list of cargo leaving the port. Was there anything too disgusting or strange to inspect?

"No garbage," he muttered.

Brian grinned. "I don't mind those inspections, as long as there's a new guy to do it."

He read the eclectic list of cargo, then grinned. "Produce," he said triumphantly.

"What?"

"Beets, cabbages, whatever is being shipped out. Is it in small boxes or big bins?"

Brian frowned. "Good question. I'll have to ask. But you're right. If it's big bins, they could store the weapons in the middle. Small boxes stacked inside larger ones could hide a false bottom." He shook his head and swore. "I'll check it out, boss, and get back to you."

"Do it fast. We've heard rumors of another weapons delivery due to go out by the end of the month."

"Sure thing." Brian rose and left the office.

David put down the papers. If he wasn't right, if they were using some other method, then he and his team were going to have to figure it out.

Brian returned to his office and stuck his head in. "Hey, I didn't know you were married. She's beautiful enough that I can see why you keep her under wraps."

"What are you talking about?"

"The woman with Ainsley. Is that your wife and kid?"

"No."

Even as he spoke, David pushed to his feet and headed out the door. There was only one reason Ainsley would bring Liz here to his office and not take her directly to the embassy. Something had gone wrong.

He walked down the main corridor and turned right. When he entered Ainsley's office, the agent hung up the phone.

"I was just calling you," she said.

Liz sat on one of the chairs in front of Ainsley's desk. She had Natasha in her arms. The baby squealed when she saw him and held out her arms. Liz looked up and tried to smile, but there were tears in her eyes. Tears and fear.

He took the chair next to Liz's and reached for the baby. Natasha snuggled close as he held her against his chest.

"What happened?"

"I have to s-stay," she said, her voice quivering. "The judge didn't waive the ten-day waiting period for Natasha, but he d-did for everyone else."

She brushed away her tears, even as more spilled onto her cheeks.

"It's a giant mess," Ainsley told him. "Somebody got to the judge. I'm sure of it. He cleared all the other families, but not only does Liz have to wait out the ten days, the judge specifically said Natasha couldn't leave the country."

Liz looked at him. "I don't understand. Where would I take her? I can't leave without a visa."

But David got it. Anger tightened his jaw. "What he's saying is that you can't take her to the American embassy for the next ten days."

At Liz's look of confusion, Ainsley leaned toward her. "It's considered American soil."

The bastard was trying to keep them in the open, David thought grimly. So Natasha would be an easier target.

"Any other restrictions?" he asked.

"Liz has to check in with the orphanage every day," Ainsley told him. "*With* the baby."

Of course. That would get her out of the hotel. Make her vulnerable. Damn whoever was behind this.

He shifted Natasha so he could see her face. Her wide blue eyes gazed back at him with complete trust. She had three fingers in her mouth and happily sucked away.

"We're going to keep you safe," he promised the baby.

"Can you?" Liz asked. "I'm not sure I can make it for ten days. What will they try?"

"We can't know," David told her, "but you're not going to have to worry. I'll take care of everything. First, we're going to get you out of that hotel. While I'm taking care of that, Ainsley, I want you to get started on tracking these people down."

She nodded. "I'll start talking to contacts and find out what I can."

He knew what she was thinking. If they could figure out why *this* baby was so special, they would be closer to figuring out who wanted her.

"I appreciate your help," he said.

"Just doing my job."

David turned his attention to Liz who stared at him with a mixture of hope and desperation.

"Come on," he said gently. "We'll go back to the hotel so you can collect your things, then you'll stay with me."

"Won't they find me there?" she asked.

"They shouldn't." Not for a few days at least. "Because of what I do over here, my address is kept secret.

If they start digging to look for it, they'll come up with false addresses that will take them all over the city."

"Okay." She rose and swallowed. "You're being so good to me."

He was about to repeat Ainsley's statement that he was just doing his job when he realized this was about more than that. He cared about Liz and Natasha. He wanted to keep them safe, not only because it was the right thing to do, but because they mattered.

Given the choice, he would have preferred Liz and Natasha to leave on the midnight flight so they could get home safely. But a part of him couldn't regret that they were going to be around longer.

Liz waited in the hallway while David went into the hotel room to make sure no one was waiting to grab her. He hadn't said as much, but what other reason could there be for having her stand back by the stairs?

He stepped out a few seconds later and smiled. "Everything looks fine. Let's finish getting you packed."

She'd already moved out of her temporary room that morning, so all that was left was to collect her toiletries and the rest of the baby supplies. David took Natasha from her, allowing her to work quickly and more easily.

Liz moved automatically, picking up a sweater and folding it, checking the bathtub for shampoo and the nightstand drawer for a book. She felt as if she were moving through water and seeing everything from a distance. Her arms and legs seemed heavy and irresponsive.

Maybe she was in shock. A part of her couldn't believe this was happening. It wasn't fair or right or even comprehensible.

Natasha giggled. Liz glanced up and saw David holding her in the crook of his arm and tickling her tummy. The baby laughed.

Under the circumstances, both she and Natasha were incredibly lucky. Without David to help them, to lean on, she didn't think she'd get through this.

Until a week ago they hadn't seen each other in almost five years, and that meeting hadn't been an entire day. Yet she felt as if she'd known him forever. He made her feel safe and with all that was going on in her life, safety seemed like a miracle.

"Knock, knock." Maggie stepped into the room. She nodded at David and turned to Liz. "How are you holding up?"

Liz didn't know how to answer the question. "Can I get back to you?" she asked at last.

The social worker smiled. "I know it seems really overwhelming, Liz, but sometimes the judges insist on the waiting period. There's nothing we can do about it except wait out the time. I don't want you to worry. I'll stay here with you until it's time to fly home."

"You don't have to do that."

"Actually I do. I need to be at the orphanage when you check in each day." She glanced at the open suitcase on the bed. "After what happened last night, I was thinking maybe we should change hotels, but you seem to be ahead of me on that."

"I'll handle Liz and Natasha's living arrangements for the next ten days," David said. "What are the rules for her visits to the orphanage? I'd prefer to avoid a set time."

Maggie frowned slightly. Liz thought maybe she would try to protest David's intervention, but instead she said, "I guess whatever is convenient for the two of you. I'll be there most of the day."

"Good. We want to avoid patterns."

Patterns? Liz had the sudden sense of being dropped into a badly written spy movie.

All this was too much. She wanted to collapse on the bed and pull the covers over her head. Instead she forced herself to finish packing.

When she was done, Maggie crossed to her and gave her a hug. "I'll be here if you need me," she said. "I've also made additional copies of Natasha's paperwork. I have one file with me in the lockbox and I took another set to the American embassy. I don't want you to worry. This will all be fine."

"I know. Thanks."

Liz said the words because they were expected, but she didn't believe them even for a second.

After Maggie left, David put Natasha in the crib. Then he took Liz's hands in his and stared into her eyes.

"Tell me what you're thinking," he said.

"You don't want to know."

"Yes, I do."

His concern was nearly more than she could handle. She wanted to throw herself into his arms and make this trouble all go away. She wanted to be magically transported home, with all this behind her.

"I'm okay."

"You're not a very good liar."

She sighed. "Normally that's a good thing."

"It still is. I need you to hang on for another couple of hours and then you can collapse. Can you do that?"

She had a feeling she would be better at the collapsing than the hanging on, but she nodded.

"Here's the plan," he said. "We're going to take Natasha over to my apartment. But we're not going to drive there directly just in case someone is watching us. In the meantime, a member of my staff will come here and get your luggage. It will be taken to the embassy, then I'll collect it later."

Good precautions, she thought, wishing they weren't necessary.

"What about all the baby supplies?" she asked.

"They'll be brought with the luggage. Don't worry about the crib. My landlady has grandchildren and she's already offered to loan us the one she uses. It should be in my place by the time we arrive."

He urged her to sit in the chair, then he crouched in front of her. "I'm going to say something, Liz, and I want you to listen very carefully. I know you want to adopt a baby. You've connected with Natasha and she's a great kid, but you don't have to follow through with this. You could simply take her back to the orphanage and get on the midnight flight home."

She stared at him, unable to believe what he was saying. Her heart nearly stopped beating as adrenaline pumped into her body. "No! I can't leave her. They would take her away. No! She's mine. I love her."

She started to push out of the chair. David rose and pulled her against him.

"It's okay," he said, brushing his lips across her forehead. "Shh. I'm sorry. I wanted to make sure *you* were sure."

Tears filled her eyes. "Don't take my baby away."

"I won't. I swear. I'll do everything I can to keep the two of you safe. Do you trust me?"

She understood why he'd done what he'd done, even if she didn't like it. But trust was another matter. She was willing to trust David with her life, and Natasha's.

She nodded.

"Then let's go."

The next two hours passed in a blur. They left the hotel in a cab. David insisted they leave the car seat behind so they would be able to move faster. By the Kremlin, they left the cab and walked around to the ticket booths, where they picked up a second cab. From there, they seemed to travel halfway to the center of the earth before emerging in a clean, bright metro station.

"This way," David said, leading her to the right platform.

She hurried after him.

He managed both Natasha and the heavy diaper bag. Liz only had to worry about herself. Obviously the man kept in good shape. She hoped they wouldn't have to run for it—if so, she would be left behind.

They changed trains twice, then emerged onto a quiet, tree-lined street where a black car waited. They got into it and were driven into an underground parking lot. Two sets of stairs, a long corridor and an elevator ride later, they were in front of David's apartment.

She looked around in confusion. "I don't understand. How did we get here? Your apartment doesn't have underground parking, does it?"

"Nope."

He opened the front door and ushered her inside. When he'd secured the lock, he popped open a panel and typed in a code on a keypad to activate a security system. Liz had the feeling that many things were not as they had first seemed.

"So how did we get here?" she asked.

"There's an underground passageway from a parking lot on the other side of the block. We'll use it while you're here so no one sees us coming or going from this building."

She was both relieved and exhausted. "I don't know what to think."

"You don't have to."

He led the way into the bedroom and opened a door. Instead of leading her into a closet or the bathroom, she found herself in a small office. A beautiful, ornate crib stood in the center of the room.

"Compliments of Mrs. P.," he said.

"Who?"

"My landlady. She oversees the building. Her mother was American, and now Mrs. P. works for the embassy."

He smiled. "She has a real last name, but I can't begin to pronounce it. Mrs. P. also told me she would leave a portable playpen in the living room."

He shifted Natasha to his left arm and moved close to Liz. "You look exhausted. I know you haven't been sleeping. I'm going to call Mrs. P. and have her come look after Natasha for the rest of the afternoon so you can get some rest."

She wanted to protest, but she couldn't seem to form the words. The thought of sleep was too tempting.

"Are you sure she's not one of them?" she asked.

"Yes. You don't have to worry. I need to get back to the office for a few hours, but I'll be back around seven. Will you be all right?"

She nodded.

"Good. Let me go get Mrs. P. so the two of you can meet."

Forty minutes later David walked back into his office. He'd introduced Liz and his landlady, then had headed back to work. He had his regular assignments to deal with, along with checking in with Ainsley to follow up on what she'd found out.

His message light blinked. He punched the numbers into the phone to retrieve messages, then sat down in his chair. Seconds later, he was standing again, listening to Ainsley's voice.

"David, page me when you get this message. I heard from one of my sources that a teenage prostitute was found murdered last night. It's crazy to think she might be involved with Liz and Natasha, but I remember Liz mentioning a teenager helping out at the orphanage. Didn't you say she was missing? I'll wait to hear from you."

He pushed in the numbers for Ainsley's pager on his cell phone even as he raced toward the stairs. The agent called him back right away.

"Where are you?" he asked.

"Heading for the morgue. Did you meet this girl? Can you identify her?"

David reached the parking level and headed for his car. "Yes. I'll be right there."

The morgue was an old building on a street of old buildings. The inside had been modernized, but no amount of remodeling could erase the smell of decades of death.

David met Ainsley by the reception desk.

"What did you find out?" he asked.

"Not much. The girl's between fifteen and seventeen. No family. Her body was found floating in the river this morning. She'd been stabbed. It could have been done by an angry customer. They'll perform the autopsy tomorrow."

He followed her deep into the building, then waited to view the body. He hadn't spent much time with Sophia, but Liz had fondly spoken of her. Of how she'd cared about Natasha and looked out for her. Had that caring been more than the concern of an involved volunteer? Had Sophia been the baby's mother and had she been killed because of the relationship?

"They're ready," Ainsley told him.

He followed her into a large white room with a row of metal body lockers against the far wall. A technician, a small man with glasses, glanced around nervously, then opened one of the lockers and rolled out a sheet-covered body. The man folded back the sheet to expose the girl's head and bare shoulders.

Her face was bloated, her features distorted, but David knew he'd never seen this girl before. Her face was round, her hair blond and curly, and there was an old scar on her cheek.

"It's not Sophia," he said flatly.

Which meant they may never know who she was or why she'd been killed.

He and Ainsley left the morgue together. As they paused by their cars, she sighed. "Now what?"

"Let's see if we can find Sophia. Maybe she has some answers. Send someone by the orphanage to get as much information as they have, then we'll start looking."

"If she's a teenage prostitute, we don't have a prayer of finding her."

"Maybe we'll get lucky."

"You think she's connected?" Ainsley asked.

"There's enough of a chance that we have to try."

"Okay. I'll get right on it and report back as soon as I know something."

David headed for his car. He would return to the office for a while, then he would go home where Liz was waiting.

Liz. She'd been through hell and there was more to come. He was determined to do his damnedest to keep her safe from everything. Even himself.

Liz woke to the sound of soft singing in a language she didn't recognize. She blinked in the filtered light and tried to place herself. The room was vaguely familiar but not immediately so. In the back of her mind, a feeling of disquiet warned her of trouble when her memory returned. Her body ached from not enough rest and too much stress. But where was she?

And then she put the pieces together—the judge's refusal to let Natasha and her leave the country, the bizarre James-Bond-like trip through the city to arrive at David's apartment without anyone knowing she and the baby were there. David's careful concern, his insistence that she rest while his landlady, a woman also employed by the embassy, looked after Natasha.

Liz sat up and swung her legs over the edge of the bed so her feet touched the floor. It was after six. She'd been asleep for nearly two hours. All she wanted was to curl up and rest until morning, but that wasn't an option.

She stood and made her way to the large bathroom. After washing her face and brushing her teeth, she smoothed back her hair and walked into the living room.

Mrs. P., a tiny woman with gray-white hair and laughing brown eyes, sat in a large wing chair. She sang softly as Natasha finished her bottle.

Mrs. P. looked up and smiled. "I've been telling her

Russian fairy stories. They are different from what you were told. Darker, but with good life lessons."

She murmured something in Russian and set the empty bottle on the end table by the chair.

"What a good baby," she said as she shifted Natasha onto her shoulder and patted her back. "Very smart."

Liz grinned. "How can you tell?"

"I know these things."

Natasha gave a very unladylike burp.

"The little one agrees," Mrs. P. said. "See? She's *very* smart."

The older woman stood and handed the baby to Liz.

"I left some food in the refrigerator. Mr. Logan isn't one to shop for himself." She tsked affectionately. "A single man like him. He needs a wife."

Not exactly a direction Liz wanted to go.

"Thank you for looking after Natasha. You're very kind."

Mrs. P. smiled. "It was no trouble. I'm in the other apartment on this floor. If you need me, come and knock on my door. Except for my trips to the market, I'm always here."

She gave a wave and let herself out.

Liz crossed to the kitchen.

A bowl of apples sat in the middle of the small table. In the refrigerator she found potatoes, hamburger, carrots, beets along with milk and cheese. Three loaves of bread nestled together on the counter.

Liz considered the ingredients on hand and the possibility that David wouldn't phone to let her know what time he would be home.

"Obviously not time for a soufflé," she told Natasha. "Your great-grandmother might have been Russian, but my college roommate's family was English. I think we have all the ingredients for shepherd's pie."

An hour later the entrée had been put together. All that was needed was some time in the oven to reheat the casserole and a couple of seconds under the broiler to brown the mashed potatoes. Liz gave Natasha a bath, then stretched out in the oversize brocade wing chair with the baby on her chest. The book of fairy tales was written in Russian, but Liz showed her daughter the pictures and made up her own stories based on the simple drawings. By seven-thirty, the baby had drifted to sleep.

Liz meant to put her in the crib, but she must have dozed off herself because the next thing she knew someone was lightly stroking her cheek and murmuring her name.

She liked both the contact and the voice, and she turned her head toward the touch so that a finger brushed across her mouth. The sensual caress made her eyes open.

David leaned over her. "How are you doing?" he asked.

"Good. Better." She started to sit up and realized Natasha was still stretched across her midsection.

"I'll take her," he said as he carefully lifted the baby into his arms. "Is her bed made?"

"Yes."

Liz had done that before her first nap.

She stood and stretched, then walked into the kitchen where she turned on the stove and washed her hands.

David wandered in a few minutes later. He'd left his briefcase in the living room, but carried a bottle of wine.

"Spanish," he said. "One of my favorites. I thought I could order from a local restaurant and we could—" He paused as she pulled the casserole out of the refrigerator and slipped it into the oven.

"You're not expected to cook for me," he told her.

"You've done nothing but look out for me since I arrived in Moscow. Now I've invaded your home. Cooking is the least I could do."

"No one's cooked for me in ages. I'm not going to say no."

"Good. Because refusing dinner would make me really crabby."

"Then I'll say thank you and leave it at that." He opened a drawer and pulled out a corkscrew. "How are you feeling?"

"Okay as long as I don't think about what's going on. If I start down that path, though, I get scared and confused, and panic isn't that far behind."

"Then I suggest we don't talk about it tonight. Let's just relax. You're safe, we're taking care of things. Nothing more can be done until morning. Fair enough?"

She nodded, then accepted the glass of wine he offered her.

"We've got about thirty minutes until dinner," she said.

He led the way into the living room where they settled on the sofa. Liz sipped the red wine. It was dry, but a little sweet and went down very easily.

"I haven't had all that much to eat today," she said with a grin. "It wouldn't take much to get me drunk."

"Don't tempt me," he teased. "I like the idea of you drunk."

"You don't know what I do under the influence."

"I'm willing to take the chance."

She laughed. Yes, there were dangers lurking in the city, and problems to be solved and risks everywhere. But for tonight she felt safe and comfortable. She was determined to enjoy every second of her time in David's company.

"Okay, but don't say I didn't warn you," she told him.

He stretched out his arm along the back of the sofa. They were close enough that his hand rested behind her shoulders. She felt his fingers tangle in her hair.

"I remember thinking you were amazingly beautiful," he said quietly. "After I left five years ago. I would recall our afternoon and evening together and tell myself you couldn't be as pretty as I thought. Then I saw you at that party at the embassy and I knew I'd been wrong. You were even more beautiful than the image in my brain."

She ducked her head. "Nice, but not necessary."

"You don't think you're attractive?"

"Sure, but there's a lot of space between pretty and beautiful."

"You own all of it."

"Thank you."

"So tell me about the men in your life. Why are you adopting a child on your own?"

She looked at him and raised her eyebrows. "Not even a subtle transition."

"Did there need to be?"

"Apparently not." She sipped her wine. "I've dated and been involved, but I've never married. Finding Mr. Right seemed less pressing than adopting a baby, so I went ahead with it and here I am."

"Why haven't you married?"

"I could ask you the same question."

"Go ahead, as soon as you answer mine."

Liz set her glass on the coffee table, angled toward him and leaned against the back of the sofa.

"I have a whole list of reasons I usually give," she said.

"Are any of them the truth?"

"A few. They satisfy curiosity."

He nodded. "You've been busy with your career. Right now you have different priorities. You don't want to compromise and you haven't met anyone worth getting excited about."

"Impressive. You've had the same conversation."

"My mother," he admitted. "She'd determined to see me happily married. So, Liz, what's the real, deep, dark, secret reason?"

"Why does it have to be a secret?"

"Because you've prepared all the other platitudes to keep the masses happy."

She laughed. "You do have a way with words."

"I have a way with a lot of things. Quit ducking the question."

She'd never much talked about her past, but with David, she found herself wanting to share the important bits. For some reason, she thought he would understand.

"My parents were very much in love," she said quietly. "They were each other's world. Looking back, I can see they shouldn't have had a child. I was only in the way, keeping them from being alone together."

"That's rough."

She shrugged. "I don't think they meant to hurt me. I always had my grandmother and she loved me enough for five people."

"That's worth something," he told her as he wove his fingers in her hair.

"I agree. I've let go of the past and moved on...sort of. My parents were kind people, just interested only in each other. Then my father died in a car accident. I was seven and devastated, but my mother..." Liz closed her eyes as she remembered her mother's loud sobbing, how she'd keened like a wild animal night after night.

"She never accepted, never recovered. Eventually she just died. The doctors couldn't figure out why, but my grandmother and I knew it was because her heart had been broken."

"Is that your deep, dark secret?" he asked. "That if you love someone it will be so completely that you won't be able to survive without him?"

She'd never articulated her views before, but now she realized that was exactly the problem.

"Yes. I don't want to be like that. I don't want to ever love too much or too deeply. I want to have more in my life."

"So do it. Love differently. Why would you close off that part of your life simply because your parents got it wrong?"

"If you're going to apply logic, there's no way I want to have this conversation."

"Sorry," he said, and put down his wineglass. "Love is worth the effort."

"So speaks the man who lives alone."

"Good point."

"So why haven't you married?" she asked. "What is your deep, dark secret?"

"That I want you," he said, even as he pulled her close and kissed her.

Ten

Liz found herself leaning forward, even as she heard a voice whispering that this was all a mistake. Look what had happened the last time she and David had made love. They'd both been shaken by the experience and run for the hills. Did she want that again? Did she really want to be swept away by the moment and the man and not give any thought to the consequences?

Honestly, yes, she thought as she gave herself over to the tender brush of his mouth on hers. She knew she was reacting to both the uncertainty of her world and David's drive to keep her safe, as much as the heat that began low in her belly and flared out in all directions. He was her only constant, her only hope. When that fact combined with the warmth of his mouth, the scent of his skin and the way he brushed his fingers against her neck, was it so very wrong to give in?

He pulled back slightly. "Now what was the question?"

She blinked. Had there been a question? "I don't remember."

"Good." He kissed her cheek, her forehead, her nose,

then her jaw. From there it was a short journey to her neck where he nibbled and licked and made her squirm in her seat.

"Are you enjoying this or thinking it's a bad idea?" he asked in a low voice, his breath warm against her damp skin.

"I'm mostly enjoying," she admitted.

"Should I stop?"

Should he? It was the best plan. Sensible, mature, the one that wouldn't get her into trouble later.

She shifted closer and wrapped her arms around him. "As long as one of us remembers to turn off the oven so dinner doesn't burn, no."

He laughed. "Fair enough. Let's take care of that first."

He stood and pulled her to her feet. As he put an arm around her waist, he urged her toward the kitchen. With a flick of his wrist, he turned off the stove. Then he cupped her face in his hands and kissed her.

She parted for him and caught her breath at the first stroke of his tongue. She felt on fire and instantly ready. Passion called and she wanted to give in right that minute. Only being naked and giving and taking would ease the ache inside of her.

"More," she breathed, and began to tug on his suit jacket.

He shrugged out of it, not seeming to care when it landed on the kitchen floor. He loosened his tie and removed it. She pulled off her T-shirt.

He groaned low and moved closer. One hand rested

on her waist, the other settled on her breast where his long fingers caressed her curves and his thumb teased her already tight nipple.

"Yes," she whispered, wanting him to touch her everywhere and make her feel alive and out of control. She arched toward him, rubbing her belly against his erection.

Hard and thick and ready, she thought. The insistent pressure against her stomach made her own insides cry out in anticipation. She wanted more—bare skin against bare skin, his thickness stretching her, filling her, even as they kissed and grabbed and took.

He slid his hand from her waist to her back where he unfastened her bra with an ease that left her breathless. She shimmied out of the garment and let it fall.

He didn't miss a beat. One hand covered her breast again, this time warm skin on warm skin, as he lowered his head and took her other nipple in his mouth.

Her legs trembled and she had to hang on to him to keep from falling in a heap at his feet.

It was good. Better than good. It was amazing. With each flick of his tongue, each pull of his lips, she felt an answering clenching between her legs. She knew she was wet and swollen. The only thing that stopped her from urging him to take things further right away was how good everything felt. She wanted more, but she wanted what she had right now. Aroused yet frustrated, she nibbled her way along his shoulder and licked at his hot skin.

He groaned. His arousal flexed. His teeth grated

lightly against her nipple and she had to choke back a scream.

"Take me," she breathed, dropping her hand between them and rubbing his length. Up and down and up and down until his breathing was as fast and heavy as her own.

"Touch me," she begged.

He took her at her word and unfastened her jeans. She pushed them down, kicking off her sandals as she went. Then she was naked and he dropped to his knees.

She had less than a heartbeat of warning before he parted her thighs and pressed his mouth against her center. The intimate contact nearly sent her tumbling. She had to hang on to the counter to keep from collapsing.

He licked the length of her, then moved leisurely along her flesh until he found that single point of pleasure. When she sucked in her breath in response to his touch, he chuckled against her.

But his humor faded as he settled into a steady pace—one designed to make her entire body tremble as her muscles tensed and her need for him grew.

It was too much. It was amazing, she thought hazily, still clinging to the tile to stay upright. She couldn't come like this, but she wasn't sure she could stop herself. Not when he inserted a single finger inside of her and curled it slightly so he seemed to stroke that one place in tandem with the magic of his tongue.

And then she could no more stop her release than she could stop the seasons. She gasped once, then twice and called out his name as her body shuddered with pleasure. Wave after wave rippled through her, and still he touched her, steadily, lightly, dragging every ounce of it from her, moving his finger in and out as the contractions went on for what felt like hours.

At last she stilled. He straightened and before she could say anything, he picked her up in his arms and carried her to the sofa in the living room.

She lay there, half sitting, half lying, as he ducked into the bedroom, only to return a couple of seconds later with a condom in hand.

She watched him move as he shucked his trousers, socks and boxers. When he was naked, she reached out to stroke him. So smooth, so hard. Mesmerized, she reached forward to press her lips against the very tip of him. She flicked lightly with her tongue and he moaned.

When she would have done more, he pulled back and opened the wrapper of the condom.

"I'd rather be inside you," he said.

"Yes." Because that was where she wanted him. Deep. Filling her over and over until her body surrendered again.

He sat next to her and urged her to straddle him. She'd never made love this way but whatever awkwardness she might have felt quickly faded when she lowered herself onto his waiting thickness.

He filled her perfectly, she thought as she sank down until their thighs touched. From this angle, he rubbed her most sensitive places.

The second time she moved up and down she felt her

eyes flutter closed. On the third, she sighed. Then he slipped one hand between her thighs and rubbed his thumb against that single spot.

Her muscles clenched. She braced herself on his shoulders and moved faster. Up and down, pleasing them both.

"Look," he breathed.

She forced her eyes open and saw him watching her. He glanced down and she followed his gaze. Her breasts bounced with each thrust. His hand was between her legs. She could feel as well as see and it was too much. She arched back as her climax claimed her again.

Under her, he stiffened, pushed up and cried out. She felt his tenseness, his release, and they came together in a tangle of bodies and heat and pleasure.

Later, when they'd dressed and cuddled together on the sofa to wait for the dinner to finish heating, David studied Liz carefully.

"What?" she asked, reaching for the wine she'd abandoned in favor of their lovemaking. "Why are you looking at me like that?"

"I'm wondering about regrets," he said. "Do you have any?"

She tucked her long hair behind her ears and sighed. "No. Do you?"

He shook his head. The last time they'd done this, they'd both felt awkward afterward. She'd headed back to her hotel as soon as she'd dressed, and he hadn't minded her leaving.

Too much, too fast, he thought, remembering his uneasiness. But now… Instead of wanting Liz farther away, he wanted her closer. Connected.

"Are you okay with what we did?" she asked.

"Completely."

"Good." Her lips curved up in a smile. "It would be a serious drag if I were feeling all snuggly and close and you couldn't wait to show me the door."

"Not a chance."

Their gazes locked and he felt something flicker between them. Not just the sexual attraction that was always there, but something more, something significant.

Caring? He knew that Liz mattered more than anyone had in a long time. He enjoyed spending time with her and Natasha. He supposed that the thought of a kid should have had him running for the hills, but it didn't. Did that have something to do with knowing she was leaving in a few days, or had he bonded with Natasha, too?

"So if neither of us wants to bolt, I guess we've entered a whole new world," she said quietly.

"Agreed."

Emotions swirled through him, but he didn't try to name any of them. It was enough to feel something for Liz. A nameless bonding. In the end she would leave and he would let her, but for now they could pretend that this was all real and that they had more than the next few days.

Everett fingered the note in his hands. He'd come into his office that morning to find it waiting for him. Even as he read it over and over, he couldn't believe it was anything but a cruel joke. Yet here he was, hopeful and eager.

He glanced down at the square of paper. Large, looping handwriting filled the sheet. "I thought maybe we could have lunch together today—12:15 work for you?"

Nancy had signed her name, then finished it off with a happy face.

He liked the happy face. The quick drawing made him smile as he tried to convince himself she'd meant what she'd said about them having lunch. He couldn't stop his insecurity. Sure, she'd stopped by his table and talked to him a couple of days ago, but that didn't mean anything. What would a wonderful, pretty woman like her see in a guy like him?

He shoved the paper into his pocket and turned to head back to his office when the elevator doors opened and Nancy stepped out.

Her brightly colored scrubs brought out the green in her hazel eyes. Her brown hair looked shiny and bouncy and there was a happy eagerness in her smile that made his heart thunder.

"Everett," she said when she reached him. "You got my note?"

He nodded, too amazed and thrilled to speak.

"Good. I got scared after I left it. You know, that maybe you were busy or didn't really want to have lunch with me."

He stared at her. "Why wouldn't I want to? You're perfect!"

She laughed and ducked her head. "Trust me, I'm not at all, but you're sweet to say so."

When she looked back at him, he saw something in her big eyes. Something like interest and maybe affection. His chest swelled with pride. Maybe she *did* like him. Maybe she thought he was special.

"Ah, would you like to get some lunch?" he said, motioning to the entrance to the cafeteria.

"That would be great."

They went through the line together and collected their food. Everett paid for both their lunches, even though Nancy tried to pay for her own. He liked that she didn't assume he would take care of things. It made him want to do more for her.

They found a quiet table by the window and sat down. When he pulled his chair in, his knee bumped hers. He jerked back and apologized. She gave him that warm smile, the one that made his stomach flip and his throat get tight.

"It's been one of those mornings," she said as she dug into her salad. "Four billion things to do and not nearly enough time."

"Four billion seems like a lot."

She laughed. "Okay, maybe it was only three billion. I love nursing, you know, helping people, especially kids, but sometimes I get exhausted. I envy you your job, working with numbers and stuff, but math was never my thing."

"Accounting isn't exactly math," he said. "It's more about being organized and keeping things together."

She wrinkled her nose. "Another failing of mine. Whatever minor talent I have for that I use up at work." She glanced around, as if checking to make sure they weren't overheard, then she leaned toward him. "Will you think less of me if I tell you I can't balance my checkbook?"

He was surprised, but tried not to show it. "Do you have trouble with it? Would you like me to help?"

She sighed. "I would love to but I'm terrified that if you saw how truly messed up I am at the whole finance thing, you'd run screaming in the other direction."

"That would never happen," he promised.

"You say that now…"

"No, Nancy. I mean it."

"Wow." She stared at him. "You're quite the guy, Everett."

"Thank you. I think you're special, as well."

As soon as he spoke the words, he wanted to call them back. What if Nancy hadn't meant that he was special? What if she thought he was weird, or anal, or just too uptight? But instead of looking uncomfortable, she bit her lower lip and blushed.

"Thank you," she murmured.

Everett suddenly felt as if he could take on the world. Nancy liked him. He didn't know how that had happened or why he was suddenly so lucky. He just knew that he didn't want to do anything to mess this up. Not when for the first time in his life he sensed…potential.

"This is fun," he said. "We should do it again."

Nancy gave him a smile. "I'd like that very much," she told him.

David left early the next morning so he could get his work done and still get home in time to take Liz and Natasha to the orphanage. They'd discussed going in the late afternoon today, then at a different time tomorrow.

Liz dangled the plastic baby keys in front of Natasha and smiled when her daughter reached for them.

"Good girl," she said. "You're doing so well."

She handed her the keys and watched as Natasha stared at them. Sometimes, when it was quiet like this, or when she was with David, she could relax and enjoy her life. But then reality rushed in and she began to worry about what might happen and then it was tough to breathe. She had to fight against the need to run for cover and remind herself that she was in a foreign country. The regular rules no longer applied.

She stretched out on the blanket, next to Natasha, and rubbed the baby's tummy. "What are we going to do?" she asked, keeping her voice light so as not to upset the child. "David is wonderful and I trust him to keep us safe. It's just hard not to worry."

She smiled at the baby. "You're much smarter than Mommy, aren't you? You go with the flow."

Had the stakes been even a little less dramatic, going with the flow was something Liz would have suggested for herself. But with her adoption of Natasha on the line, it was tough to be rational and relaxed.

"I know," she said, scrambling to her feet and hurrying into the bedroom. She dug through her suitcase and pulled out a sketch pad and a zipper case full of pencils.

"How about if you look pretty and I draw you?" she said as she returned to the living room. "Can you smile for Mommy?"

Liz passed the rest of morning by making sketches. After feeding Natasha formula and a little cereal, then fixing herself a sandwich, she read to the baby, then put her down for a nap. About fifteen minutes later, David walked in.

"It's me," he called as he stepped into the apartment.

Liz's mood brightened measurably and she had to fight against the urge to rush into his arms and welcome him with a kiss. She held back because the action seemed too wife-like, and while she knew he wanted her in his bed, she wasn't sure he was looking for anything else. Come to think of it, she wasn't supposed to be, either. Relationships didn't work, she reminded herself. At least, not romantic ones.

"How was your day?" David asked as he gave her a quick kiss on the cheek. "Were you able to relax at all?"

"Some. Natasha was perfect, as usual. She ate cereal with no trouble. I did some sketches of her, and then we read."

He smiled. "I'm guessing you're reading to her and not the other way around."

"Exactly. But I think she's really getting the hang of

it." She glanced at her watch. "When do you want to head to the orphanage?"

"Not for about an hour. I would like there to be more traffic. It'll make us harder to follow."

Her stomach clenched at his words. "Are you sure they'll be trying?"

"No, but better to be safe." He looked around the room. "Is she sleeping?"

"Yes. I just put her down."

"Then let her be."

He took Liz's hand and led her to the sofa. When they were seated he looked at her with enough concern to make her afraid.

"What?" she asked. "You've found out something."

"No, but I've been wondering about Sophia. You said she'd been missing."

"Right. I told Maggie and the director, but they said it happens all the time. The teenage girls who help out usually don't have any family of their own. Being around the other kids makes them feel like they're home. But when life interferes, they disappear."

"Is that what you think?"

Liz wasn't sure. "I don't know why Sophia is helping, but I don't think she disappeared because of a previous engagement. She cared too much about all the babies, but especially Natasha. It's as if—"

Liz stared at him as a thought popped into her head. "Do you think Natasha is hers?"

She wanted him to be shocked, to tell her that it wasn't possible, but instead he shrugged.

"Could be."

"No!"

She didn't want to believe that. She didn't want to know who her daughter's biological mother was.

"But if she is, will she take her back? Is she the one who talked to the judge?" Tears filled her eyes. "Is she going to take Natasha from me?"

David pulled her close and wrapped his arms around her. "Don't go there," he told her. "Even if Sophia is the baby's mother, there's no reason to worry that she's changed her mind about giving her up. Natasha is four months old. In all that time Sophia hasn't said a word to anyone. Why would she want the baby back now?"

"Because she's met me. Because I'm real and I'm taking her baby away from her."

He stroked her hair. "You're scared and I understand that, but try to think about all this logically. Sophia knew about you from your last visit. We don't know if she *is* Natasha's mother, but even if she is, she's had over a month to spirit her daughter away. Instead she stayed close and took care of her until you returned."

All Liz wanted to do was grab the baby and run, but she forced herself to be logical and listen to what David was saying. Some of it made sense.

"So where is she?" she asked.

"I don't know. I want to say it doesn't matter, but I have a feeling in my gut that says Sophia is somehow involved in all this."

"So we have to find her."

"Agreed. I have some people looking for her, but

Moscow is a huge city. She could be anywhere. She might have even left."

Maybe, but Liz wasn't convinced. Her gut told her that Sophia would stay around until Natasha was safe.

"You'll let me know what you find?" she asked.

He nodded. "Until then, try to relax as much as you can. I'm here."

Two simple words that meant so much to her. *I'm here.* So much time and effort when he could have passed her off to someone else.

"I don't know how I'm going to repay you for all you've done," she said.

"Not necessary."

"But this is more than your job."

He looked at her. "You're right. I don't usually make love with the women I'm protecting."

She felt her cheeks heating. "I didn't mean that."

"Didn't you? We've always had chemistry between us from the first. Remember what happened in Portland?"

"Every second of it. My big confession is that I'm embarrassed by how long it took me to get over you."

"I thought about you a lot, too. I kept thinking I should have brought you with me."

"And I kept thinking I should just show up on your doorstep one day." Liz knew that decision would have changed her life forever. Is that why she'd never done it? Because she was afraid of what would happen?

"Eventually I did just that," she said lightly. "Showed up with no warning."

He took her hand in his. "I'm glad you did."

"Me, too. Even under the circumstances." She laughed. "I'm going to guess that if you ever thought about us seeing each other again, there was never a four-month-old baby in the mix."

"Natasha is great, and I admire what you're doing by adopting her."

She appreciated the compliment. "You're very sweet to say that, but my reasons aren't all that noble. My grandmother's life was changed when she was adopted, and she and I talked abut the orphans over here. The seed for this was planted a long time ago."

"Still, Natasha will get a chance that a lot of kids don't get. Even though you lost your parents, you still grew up with family. When a kid doesn't have that..." He shrugged. "It's tough."

There was something in his voice. Something that made her lean toward him and ask, "Are you speaking from personal experience?"

He nodded. "I have a twin sister, Jillian. Our mother was a drug addict and left us with her mother."

Liz couldn't believe it. "You, too?"

"My story doesn't have the same happy ending as yours. Not at first, anyway. Our grandmother had a stroke and couldn't talk. She could barely care for us. Jillian and I were pretty much left to fend for ourselves. By the time the state found us, we were five. We'd developed our own language and missed out on a lot of learning opportunities. That made school a challenge."

Looking at him now, she would never think he'd had

anything but a perfect childhood. "What an amazing story."

"Because of our unique circumstances, we were put into Children's Connection instead of foster care. The theory was Jillian and I could receive better care and therapy to help us overcome our issues. I know now it was the right thing to do, but Jillian and I were terrified. We'd never seen that many other kids before. I'm not sure we'd ever left our grandmother's house and yard. Nothing made sense and we thought we were going to be separated."

She studied his face, searching for clues about his past. He was a Logan, so she'd just assumed he'd grown up in wealth and privilege. How could that not be true?

"What happened?" she asked.

"We were sent to special classes to learn how to talk. For a while the experts said we would never be normal. Then Leslie Logan came along and adopted us." He smiled. "I asked her why once. Why when there were so many normal kids around, did she pick us? She said it was because we needed her more and she wanted to be needed."

"So the Logans took you home and changed your lives?"

"That's the story." His gaze sharpened. "That's who I am, Liz. Not a Logan by birth, but the kid of a crackhead."

"Look at all you've done with your life. It's impressive."

He shook his head. "There are still dark holes and flaws."

"Because the rest of us are so perfect?" She laughed. "David, you've faced your demons and survived. In my book that means you're one step ahead of the rest of us."

"You don't understand."

"I understand perfectly." She looked at her watch and sighed. "We can't stay here forever. What time do you want to leave?"

He hesitated, as if he wanted to say more, then checked the time. "Another fifteen minutes."

"Then I'd better get Natasha's things together."

"The baby is paid for," the Stork said, his voice low and angry. "The parents were very specific about the age and sex and coloring. Don't tell me you can't find the one baby we need."

Kosanisky swallowed. "We know where she is." Almost. She was with the American woman who was being helped by someone. The man was better than anyone Kosanisky had ever hired.

"They paid a premium of fifteen thousand dollars on top of the regular price," the Stork reminded him. "I don't want to have to give it back."

"No. You won't have to."

"I had better not. You have forty-eight hours to produce the baby. If you don't, you'll be sorry. Do I make myself clear?"

Kosanisky thought about the cold water in the river and how many disappeared into its murky depths.

Eleven

Liz and David retraced their steps to the underground parking lot, where a different car and two men were waiting for them.

"Backup," he said, introducing her to the men. One was Russian, one American. She smiled and shook hands and fourteen seconds later couldn't remember their names.

It was the fear. The dark emotion sat in her stomach and made it difficult to think or breathe or even hope. They were out there waiting. Whoever wanted Natasha. Strangers were after her baby, and she was terrified that nothing could stop them.

David drove to the orphanage using back roads and alleys. He made U-turns, circled and wove in and out of traffic. Natasha had barely stirred when Liz had put her in the car seat. Now the baby slept on, oblivious of the tension in the car.

Finally they arrived at the orphanage. The American agent stepped out and stood close as the Russian unfastened the car seat. As he handed it to Liz and David stepped onto the sidewalk, three men rushed toward them.

One second there was nothing, then the men were there. They were large and dark, and one of them had a gun.

"The baby. Now!"

The words were harsh and low, spoken with a thick accent. Even so, Liz registered the meaning. Her fear intensified. She couldn't move, could only stare at the snub barrel of the gun and know that she would die soon because she wouldn't willingly give up Natasha.

David moved next to her. Even though she didn't turn, she sensed his presence. Her heart pounded so fast, it was more a vibration than a beat. Her entire body was cold. Everything hurt.

She wasn't sure how long they stood there, practically frozen in stillness. It felt like hours but was probably less than two seconds.

Unexpectedly, David spun in a graceful movement and caught the armed man's wrist with his foot. The gun went flying. Someone big and heavy plowed into her, but instead of throwing her to the ground and taking the baby, she found herself half pushed, half carried into the orphanage. It was only when she'd burst through the doors and was able to turn around that she saw the American guy moving her deeper into the building.

"David," she gasped.

"He'll be fine."

"But there are three of them."

The man, tall and blond, grinned at her. "Don't

worry." He nodded at the car seat where Natasha stirred and blinked. "Want me to carry her?"

"No. I'm fine."

Not exactly the truth considering how hard she was shaking.

"Was David expecting trouble? Is that why he brought you along?"

"Expecting is too strong a word. He's the kind of man who likes to be prepared."

They turned a corner and saw Maggie running toward them. "I was watching for you out the window and I saw what happened. Are you all right?"

"We're fine," the man said.

Liz looked at him. "I'm sorry. I don't remember your name."

"Robert."

"Thank you for everything."

"Just doing what I was trained for."

Liz wasn't sure she wanted to know what that training usually entailed. She followed Maggie into the nursery, where she moved Natasha into a crib, then hovered over her.

"It's okay," Maggie said soothingly. "You're fine."

"But for how long?" Liz clenched her hands into fists and fought tears. "When will they be back? What happens next?"

"We find them," David said from the doorway.

Liz acted on instinct and headed for him. He pulled her close against him and hugged her tight.

"Are you all right?" he asked quietly.

"I don't have to worry about getting my aerobic workout today," she said, trying to sound normal and not sure if she succeeded.

He chuckled. "Good for you. Stay strong, Liz. It's the only way to keep the bastards from winning."

Good advice, but she wasn't sure how long she could take it. Right now she felt about as strong and impressive as melted butter.

"They get away?" Robert asked.

"Yeah. We nearly had them, but then they bolted. Dmitri went after them but I'm not expecting him to find anything." David stepped back and looked at Liz. "I'm going to leave Robert here to watch over things."

She nodded. While she would have preferred David stay with her, she knew he had a job to do.

"We'll be fine."

He smiled at her. "You're not a very good liar."

"I'm out of practice."

"There's no need for that to change. When I get back to the office, I'm going to see what I can do about contacting another judge and getting you and Natasha out of here sooner."

"I have the name of the judge we saw yesterday," Maggie said. "Would that help?"

"Yes," David said. "Thank you."

Maggie hurried off toward the office.

Yesterday? Had it really been less than twenty-four hours since she'd been told she had to stay an extra ten days? Liz felt as if she'd been living this nightmare for weeks. Complicating matters was the ache in her heart.

Of course she wanted to leave Moscow as soon as possible. She would do anything to keep Natasha safe. But what about David? Was she just supposed to walk away and never see him again?

She caught her breath. "I don't like any of this."

"You'll be fine," he promised. "Robert will be here all day, watching over Natasha. If Dmitri isn't back in the next fifteen minutes, I'll send someone else to patrol the orphanage. I want you to try to stay calm."

While she was grateful for the guards, she'd prefer to be with David. She wanted them to stay together. Was there a "them"? she wondered. Did she matter to him? What about her own feelings? Was she reacting to the situation or something more?

"I'll be in touch," he said, and kissed her cheek. "You have my number if you need to talk to me, or Robert can page me. I'll be back in a couple of hours."

She nodded and watched him go. A part of her wanted to call him back, but the sensible part of her brain warned her that she had better get used to being without David. As soon as she left Moscow, he'd be out of her life forever.

Leaving Robert standing guard over a sleeping Natasha, Liz wandered down to the office and found Maggie.

She held up a coffeepot. "Want some?"

"Sure."

Liz took a mug and filled it, then added some cream and sugar.

"I gave David the name of the judge," Maggie said as she sat behind one of the two battered desks. "I'm not sure if it will help or not."

Liz settled across from her. "Me, either, but it can't hurt. Maybe they can trace him back to the people behind all this. Maybe not. I don't know how much cooperation there is between David's office and the local police."

Maggie nodded. "I've never had trouble with an adoption before but I've talked to some other caseworkers who have. Apparently the local government isn't happy about the number of children being adopted by Westerners. They seem to feel it makes them look bad—like they can't look after their own children."

"But that's not the case at all. Every country has orphans."

"True." Maggie sipped her coffee. "I've heard the Russian people are very proud. I can respect that. My concern is that if the local police don't like the adoption process in the first place, I don't know how much they'll go out of their way to facilitate things."

"Good point," Liz said glumly. "Plus, they won't like the implication that there's a black market working in the area."

She took a drink of her coffee and tried not to focus on the negative. If she thought about it too much, she would start crying and what would that accomplish?

"You said other caseworkers had had problems. Anything like this?"

Maggie shook her head. "I was talking more about

missing paperwork or sick babies. No one else has ever been held up right outside the orphanage."

Liz didn't want to think about the men and the gun. "I wonder how they found us. David took back roads the whole way. He turned and backtracked. It was like being in the middle of a Hollywood chase scene."

"The judge made it clear you had to check in here every day. Maybe they were waiting for you."

Liz didn't like the sound of that. Bad men lurking outside the orphanage? Thank God, David had left Robert to guard Natasha.

Just then the other man who had been in the car with them walked in. He was tall and muscular, with Slavic features. When Liz turned to him, he shook his head.

"I lost them," he said in his thickly accented voice. "David asked me to patrol the grounds and the building." He looked at Maggie. "You need to see my ID?"

She looked uncomfortable, but nodded, then studied the badge he showed her.

"I know you're here to keep Liz and Natasha safe," Maggie said. "Please remember there are a lot of children running around, so don't attack everything that runs out of a closet."

The man smiled, flashing white teeth. "I be careful," he promised.

There was something about his voice, something low and seductive. It took Liz a second to realize he was staring at Maggie in a way that had nothing to do with business and everything to do with being a man in the presence of an attractive woman.

Liz glanced from one to the other. It made sense. Maggie was in her late twenties, pretty and, judging from the lack of rings on her fingers, single.

Liz rose. "I'm going to stretch my legs for a bit before Natasha wakes up. Is it all right if I walk outside?"

Dmitri nodded. "Stay within the grounds of the orphanage."

"Not a problem."

She hadn't planned on leaving. Besides, from what she could tell, the bad guys weren't interested in her.

She left her coffee by the sink and stepped into the hallway. Due to circumstances beyond her control, she'd been trapped indoors for the past couple of days. She couldn't wait to enjoy the warm and sunny afternoon.

After turning left into the main corridor, Liz circled around to the rear of the building and stepped out into the walled-in garden. The playgrounds were all on one side. She avoided that area and walked toward the gardens.

This time of year the orphanage grew as much fresh produce as it could. Whatever was left over was frozen to provide food for the winter. She noticed a small plot of flowers against the far wall and walked in that direction.

The air was pleasant and redolent with the scent of things growing. She saw green beans and tomatoes, along with carrots, potatoes and beets. Or at least the tops of the root vegetables, along with a small wooden sign painted with a picture of what was in each row.

"Clever," she murmured. That way the older children could help and know what they were growing.

At the far end of the garden was a small shed, probably for tools and supplies. Maybe extra seeds. Liz walked around it and settled in a patch of shady lawn. She leaned against a tree trunk and stared up at the sky. So blue, she thought, so vivid. How could that sky be so perfect when things were so messed up down here? How could—

The shed door creaked. Liz stared at the battered wood and wondered if she'd imagined it. Her heart began to beat faster and she didn't know if she should stay where she was or run screaming into the main building.

Is that where those men lurked? Did they plan to attack from the garden?

She eyed the shed and wasn't sure how many of them could fit inside. Besides, here at the back of the main orphanage building there weren't even any windows until the third floor. This was not the easy way in.

Still undecided, she continued to watch the shed. The door creaked again, then Liz saw a flicker of movement. She opened her mouth to scream, only to bite back the sound when someone familiar limped into the sunlight.

"Sophia!"

Liz jumped to her feet just as the teenager saw her. Liz recognized the fear in the girl's eyes as she turned to run.

"Don't go!" Liz called after her. "Please. I want to help you."

Sophia turned slowly. Liz winced when she saw bruises on the girl's face and a large scrape on her arm.

"It's all right," Liz said, lowering her voice and making it as gentle as she could. "No one wants to get you in trouble. I've been worried about you."

"I am fine," Sophia said defiantly.

"You don't look fine." Liz studied the matted hair and gaunt face, and made an educated guess. "You look like you've been on the run. Is it because the same men who are after Natasha are after you?"

Sophia's dark eyes widened. Liz recognized her terror.

"They don't have her," Liz said quickly. "They've tried to get her, but we've managed to keep her safe."

Sophia's wary expression sharpened. "We?"

"David Logan and myself. The man I was with before. The American. He's helping me."

"You should be gone by now," Sophia said sharply. "When do you have your hearing?"

"It's a long story. Please, won't you let me help you?"

The teenager shook her head and started to limp away. Liz ached to go after her.

"Sophia, wait! I know the truth. I know you're Natasha's birth mother."

It was a long shot, but it worked. The girl froze in place.

"No. She is not mine."

But her words weren't convincing, not when she started to shake. Liz walked over and put an arm around her.

"Come inside," she said. "We'll get you cleaned up and fed. I'll talk to David and we'll find somewhere safe for you to stay."

The girl shrugged off her embrace. "Why would you help me?"

"Because I want you to be all right. You can't continue to hide out in the shed. I won't say anything, but eventually someone else will find you and then what? Please, Sophia. Come inside."

The girl nodded. Liz took her arm and led her into the building. Dmitri met them at the back door.

"Who is she?" he asked roughly.

"A friend of mine. David knows about her."

The man didn't look convinced, but allowed them passage. Liz led the way to one of the private rooms in the infirmary. She left Sophia on the bed and went in search of supplies.

Maggie met her in the hall. "Dmitri told me you'd found someone outside."

"Sophia," Liz said as she collected bandages and first-aid cream. "I think she's been hiding out for a couple of days. I want to talk to her privately. Is that all right? I'm afraid she won't talk if too many people are around."

Maggie's hazel eyes darkened with compassion. "Of course. Do you think she's hungry? Let me go get a sandwich and some soup. Should you call David and tell him?"

Liz considered the question, then shook her head. "I want to get her story first. I can let him know when he gets back."

Half expecting Sophia to have bolted, she returned to the small room. The teenager still sat on the edge of the narrow bed. Her wary gaze followed Liz as she poured water into a metal bowl and set out clean cloths.

"What happened?" she asked as she took the girl's arm and examined the scrape. "It looks as if you fell off a mountain."

"I jumped out of a van."

Liz pulled up a stool and settled on it. "I'm sure you had a good reason."

She positioned Sophia's arm over the bowl, then squeezed water over the scrape. The girl winced. Working carefully, Liz washed away dirt and grit. Most of the wound had already scabbed over. She washed the cut on Sophia's face, then shivered at a circular burn on the girl's other arm.

"What caused that?" she asked.

"A cigarette."

Liz's stomach knotted. She didn't want to know any more. She didn't want to be part of this ugly world. Life had been much easier back in Portland.

She washed the burn, then asked about other injuries.

"Just bruises," Sophia said. "From when I hit the road."

"Do you think you broke something?"

"No."

"Come on." Liz led her to the bathroom. There were fresh towels by the shower. "Go ahead and get cleaned up. Maggie is preparing you something to eat. I'll find some clean clothes and then we can talk."

The teenager stared at her. "Why you so nice?"

"Because I want to help. You were there for Natasha."

Sophia's shoulders drooped. "My daughter. What else would I do?"

"A lot of people would have just walked away. You stayed to keep her safe. I want to repay you for that."

Sophia didn't look impressed. Liz tried another tack. "Who taught you English? You speak very well."

Sophia shrugged. "An old woman who lived in my building. She was British. She never said how she came to live here. She did not walk good. I helped out. She taught me English. Then she died."

"You helped her and she helped you back. That's all I want to do. I owe you."

Sophia didn't look convinced but she stopped arguing. Liz left her alone in the bathroom, then hovered outside the door until she heard the sound of running water.

She found Maggie in the small infirmary room. The social worker had brought sandwiches and soup.

"She needs clothes," Liz said. "Are there any big enough to fit her?"

Maggie smiled. "She's so tiny, I don't think it's going to be a problem. Let me go look at what we have."

She disappeared down the hall in the direction of the supply closet. Minutes later she reappeared with clean underwear, a T-shirt and two pairs of jeans in different sizes.

"Thanks," Liz said. "These should work until we get her things washed."

"What are you going to do with her?" Maggie asked. "I don't mean to be cruel, but she can't stay here."

"I know. I'll talk to David when he arrives. I'm sure there's a place she can go. If not, we'll put her up at a hotel."

Maggie looked as if she wanted to say something, but Liz grabbed the clothing and left before she could. The last thing she needed right now was the other woman explaining why it wasn't possible to save Sophia. At this point, Liz didn't care about what was possible; she wanted what was right.

Thirty minutes later Sophia had dressed, eaten and followed Liz into the nursery. The teenager approached the crib cautiously. Robert watched as she bent over Natasha's crib and smiled.

Sophia spoke softly in Russian, then lifted the baby into her arms. If Liz'd had any doubts about the girl's relationship to the child, they disappeared the second she saw her face.

Love and pain combined in an expression so fierce, Liz had to look away. Her heart clenched as she questioned her right to take Natasha away. Doubts crashed in and made her want to cry out. She forced herself to stay strong.

"We should go somewhere and talk," she said, hoping she sounded remotely normal as she spoke. "Most of the kids are outside. We could go into the playroom."

Sophia nodded and led the way. Liz followed with Robert at her side.

"What's going on?" he asked.

"Nothing. Sophia works here. She's been gone for a while and hasn't seen Natasha."

She was grateful that he accepted her explanation. She didn't want to have to go into detail about who the teenager was. Liz would rather discuss that with David.

Light filled the large playroom, filtering in through massive windows. Scarred hardwood floors showed years of use. A stone fireplace stood in the corner.

Sophia collected several blankets from a stack by the door while Liz grabbed a few floor pillows. They moved into the room and arranged the blankets and pillows on the floor. Sophia set Natasha on her stomach and sat next to the baby. Liz perched on a pillow, while Robert pulled up a chair by the door.

"Who is that man?" Sophia asked, her back to Robert, her voice low.

"He works with David. He's here to protect Natasha."

Sophia looked at her. "The baby, not you?"

Liz managed a slight smile. "Yup. They could come get me and no one would even blink."

"But you are not target."

"Exactly. Why were you?"

Sophia held out her finger to the baby who grasped it tightly. "You were right. I am her mother."

Liz nodded, not surprised to have the information confirmed. "You always worried about her so much, took care of her. I didn't realize it at first, but after you disappeared and those men tried to take her from me, I began to wonder."

Sophia sighed. "I did not mean for things to go

wrong. The man after her, Kosanisky, he is a bad man. He has power and is not afraid to hurt people."

Liz glanced at the burn on the girl's arm. "Did he do that to you?"

"Yes. When I would not bring him Natasha." Sophia looked at her. "I work for him, since I was fourteen. I am prostitute."

Liz kept her expression as passive as possible.

When she didn't speak, the teenager continued. "I have been pregnant before. I try not to be, but it is difficult. The men do not always wear condoms. With my last baby, Kosanisky told me to get rid of it. I did not want to but he beat me and then I lost the baby anyway."

Liz swallowed hard against the bile rising in her throat. She wanted to yell out her protest that such a world existed. She wanted to pull Sophia into her arms and hold her close.

"How old are you?" she asked.

"Seventeen," Sophia said flatly. "Soon I will be too old to work for him, but for now…I survive."

That wasn't survival, Liz thought. It was hell.

"With Natasha things were different," Sophia said. "Kosanisky told me to keep the baby. That he find a home for her. At first I thought he meant here, in Russia. Then I learned the babies sent to America. Rich couples pay for them. I did not like that, but I knew Natasha would be safer there. I knew I could not keep her."

Liz desperately wanted to ask if the girl had been tempted, then wondered if it were possible. How could she have a baby around if she worked as a prostitute?

What other work could she find that paid anything? She doubted Sophia had gone to school. She'd been trapped by circumstances beyond her control.

"When Natasha was born, I was told to take care of her for six weeks. Then Kosanisky would come for her." Sophia pulled a couple of pillows close and propped the baby up against them. Natasha giggled with delight.

"After a few days I knew I did not want her to be sold like dog in the market. I brought her here. Then I came myself. I wanted to see the family who would adopt her. If I did not like them, I told myself I would take her away."

"Kosanisky didn't know?" Liz asked.

"I did not tell him, but he knew. The first deal failed and I was glad. Now another couple come." She glanced at Liz and smiled again. "You came. I watched you with Natasha. I could see in your face that you love her very much. That is good. But then while you were gone Kosanisky found another couple. They wanted special baby to look a certain way. He had me take pictures of Natasha. She was what they wanted. They paid extra. He agreed and then he wanted baby."

"But you didn't have her."

"No. And I would not get her." She waved the arm with the burn. "He tried to make me. He knew she was at orphanage. And he knew about you. I would not say your name and then I got away. But he will keep coming after her. He will not stop. Ever."

Twelve

Liz returned to the playroom after calling David and telling him a bit about what had happened. He cautioned her not to say too much on the phone, so she was as vague as possible.

Sophia sat where she'd left her, holding Natasha and singing to her, which made Liz wonder if she'd overreacted in whispering to Robert that he was not to let the teenager out of the room. Maybe Sophia didn't plan to bolt.

As Liz approached, her heart constricted again. There was such love in Sophia's expression, such longing. As much as Liz loved the baby, she knew her feelings couldn't compare. She'd only known Natasha several weeks while Sophia had loved her since before her birth.

"David is on his way," she said when Sophia looked up at her. "He's good at this sort of thing. He'll know what to do."

"What is there to be done?" Sophia asked, sounding resigned. "Kosanisky wants my baby and he will not stop until he has her." She looked at Liz. "I had hoped you would get away. Once you are out of Russia, he has no power over you."

Liz didn't answer; she couldn't. Two simple words had her emotions in a death grip and wouldn't let go. *My baby.*

Of course. That was who Natasha was. Sophia's child. When Liz had thought of the girl as the baby's mother, it was a more disconnected relationship. But the two were bonded by more than biology.

"Do you want to keep her?" Liz asked, barely able to speak the words, but sure she had to.

Sophia raised her head and stared at her wide-eyed. "What?"

"Natasha. You love her. I can see that. If you want to…" She had to swallow hard before she could speak again. "I would understand if you—"

"No!"

Sophia thrust the child at her. Natasha cried out a complaint at the rough handling. Liz took her and murmured softly. Sophia scooted back a few inches.

"No," she repeated, more softly this time. "I cannot. She is better with you."

"But you love her."

The teenager shrugged. "Love will not feed her or keep her safe. You can do both."

Liz wasn't sure what to say. Sophia might be more than a decade younger, but the tired wisdom in her eyes spoke of all she'd seen, all she'd endured.

"I could help," Liz said because she had to.

Sophia picked up the terry-cloth giraffe and handed it to the baby. Natasha grasped it, then tossed it away. Sophia picked it up and gave it back to her and the baby giggled.

"I have a cousin," Sophia said, looking only at the giraffe. "She lives far away. Not in a city. She is older than me, married with three children. We write sometimes. There is a man who lives near her. A farmer. He is kind and honest and he looks for a wife. My cousin gave him my picture."

Sophia looked at Liz. "He thinks I am a good girl who has lived in an orphanage all these years. Of all he knows of me, it is the only lie. So he wants to marry me. My cousin says the work is hard, but easy when compared to what I have lived. I know she is right. What is it to milk cows or tend a garden?"

"Are you going to marry him?" Liz asked.

"Yes. When I know you and Natasha are away, I will go to my cousin and meet this man. I was a good girl once. I think I remember what to do."

Her young face hardened with determination. "My cousin says he will not beat me, that he wants someone to help him and give him children. I can do that." Her mouth curved in a sad smile. "I know many ways to please him in bed."

Liz shook her head. "It doesn't have to be like that. I can help. I want to help. Why would you marry a stranger? Sophia, there are other opportunities."

The teenager looked at her with pity. "You do not understand what it is like for someone like me. I *want* to go to the country. I want to be what I once was. Clean. Good. If I take Natasha, he will suspect and then all will be different between us. Better that I go alone. That I pretend until I become that other girl." She looked out the window. "I have to save myself."

Liz didn't want to understand. She didn't want this to be Sophia's world. But the words made sense and she knew that for the teenager, this was a chance to start over without a past.

"I will love her with all my heart," Liz said quietly. "She will want for nothing. I promise you."

Sophia continued to stare out the window. A single tear rolled down her cheek. "Yes. It is right. As she grows, you will talk of me. I would like you to be kind in what you say."

Liz nodded. She couldn't speak through her own tears.

David took the stairs to the playroom two at a time. When he stepped through the door, his agent walked over.

"The girl showed up a couple of hours ago," Robert said in a low voice. "They've been in here about ninety minutes. Talking. I didn't listen."

David nodded. Robert's instructions had been to keep Natasha in sight at all time, not eavesdrop on Liz and Sophia.

"We'll be heading out in a while," David said. "I'll need you to follow and look for a tail."

"Sure, boss."

David left him by the door and walked over to the two women. They both stood when they saw him. Liz looked pleased, but Sophia took a couple of steps back.

"You came," Liz said, sounding relieved.

He tucked her hair behind her ear and kissed Natasha's forehead. "Did you doubt me?"

"Not at all. It's just with everything going on…" She sighed. "The stress is getting to me." She turned to the teenager. "Sophia, you remember David Logan. He works at the embassy." She looked back to him. "I'm not exactly clear on what you do."

"It's better that way." He looked at Sophia. "How are you feeling?"

"Fine."

He studied the scrapes and bruises, then moved closer to inspect a round burn on the girl's arm. He recognized the shape and swore silently.

"Who did this to you?" he asked.

"Vladimir Kosanisky. I work for him."

She spoke almost angrily, her shoulders squared, her head back. The combination of wariness and defiance in her expression explained much about her relationship with Kosanisky.

"Then we'll have to get the bastard, won't we?"

Sophia relaxed a little. "Are you sure you can? He is powerful. He knows people. He pays money—not just bribes. He controls a world you know nothing about."

David motioned to the pillows and blankets on the floor. "Why don't you tell me about it?"

When they were seated, Liz brought him up to speed

on everything. Sophia filled in a few details. He made notes and listened, careful not to show any emotion, even when she admitted to being Natasha's birth mother.

Kosanisky's name was familiar. If he was in the black market baby business, Ainsley would know more. David jotted down a reminder to get in touch with her that evening. Sophia mentioned bribes and payments. That would explain the judge insisting on the ten-day waiting period.

"What do you know about Kosanisky?" he asked. "Can you give me some other names?"

"A few. Some locations. If he knows I'm talking to you, all will change."

If he knew Sophia was talking to him, David thought, she would soon be dead.

"You can't stay in town," he said.

"She's planning to move to the country," Liz told him.

"Good." He stared at Sophia. "You can go tonight."

The teenager shook her head. "I will stay until I know that Natasha is out of the country. I want her safe."

"What good is that information if Kosanisky catches you?"

She barely flinched. "I can take care of myself. He has not caught me yet."

"It's just a matter of time and we both know it." David considered his options. Could he hide her for the next nine days?

"When is the hearing?" Sophia asked. "It should be soon, yes?"

David glanced at Liz who shook her head. "I didn't

get around to telling her that." She quickly explained how the judge had forced her and Natasha to wait out the ten days.

Sophia paled. "He bought the judge. He will come after you."

"He already has," David said flatly, and told her about the attack when they entered the orphanage. "The good news is once we leave, we don't have to come back. We found another judge who agreed that it wasn't necessary to check in at the orphanage before the next hearing."

Liz picked up the giraffe Natasha had tossed on the floor. "Will he let me take her to the embassy?"

"No. Natasha still isn't allowed to leave the country until the final hearing."

She nodded. He saw her blink several times as if trying not to cry.

"At least we can find a safe place and lay low," she said, her voice thick with emotion. "That's something."

But was it enough? David wasn't sure. First he'd had to worry about Natasha and Liz. Now there was Sophia. If he could get the girl to leave town… No point in arguing that. He recognized a stubborn female when he saw one.

"I can put you up at a hotel outside of town," David told Sophia. "Provide protection. You'd still be close to Natasha and be able to know exactly when she and Liz leave the country."

The wariness returned. "Why would you help me? I am not American."

"That's not always a requirement."

Sophia studied him. "You do this for me?"

He nodded. "I would rather you left Moscow, but if you won't, this is the next best plan. I'll assign an agent to protect you."

"I can take care of myself."

He grabbed her arm and turned it so the burn caught the light. "Do you know what Kosanisky will do if he finds you? A couple of days ago a body was pulled from the river. A young woman about your age."

Sophia paled, but didn't back away. "I know," she said as she pulled her arm free. "If Kosanisky finds me, he will torture me, then he will kill me."

Liz's breath caught audibly, but David continued to stare at the teenager.

"Is that what you want?" he asked.

"I will stay until Natasha leaves the country. You cannot make me do anything else."

"Then you'll stay where I tell you and you'll have an agent to protect you. Is that clear?"

She slowly nodded.

It wasn't much of a victory, but it was the best he could expect right now.

He stood and held out his hand to Liz.

"Get Natasha's things together," he said as he pulled her to her feet. "We'll be leaving shortly. I'll speak with Maggie and explain that we don't have to check in here anymore. I'll give her a number where she can get in touch with us at any time."

Liz nodded without speaking. Her eyes were wide and she looked shell-shocked. No doubt this was as far from her regular world as she had ever been. He took a second and put his arm around her.

"You and the baby will be fine," he promised, then hoped he wasn't lying. "I'm right here."

"It's okay. I just…" She swallowed and looked at him. "I didn't know it could be like this for anyone. It's not right."

He agreed, but there wasn't much they could about it. "Sophia will be protected."

"Thank you for taking care of that."

"No problem." He kissed her lightly, then went off in search of Dmitri.

Ten minutes later, he had everything arranged. He returned to the playroom with Dmitri in tow.

He introduced the agent to Sophia. "He's your shadow," he told her. "Dmitri goes everywhere with you. Understood."

The teenager eyed the burly man with distaste. "I don't need to be watched."

"He's going to protect you, not watch you."

Dmitri spoke in Russian. "You can trust me. I won't hurt you."

Sophia's gaze narrowed as she answered in the same language. "I trust no man."

Dmitri shook his head. "I have a sister your age. You're still a little girl."

David had the feeling Sophia hadn't been a little girl in a long time.

Dmitri grinned. "Besides, I'm too handsome. I have many women to please me. I don't need any more."

Sophia surprised David by smiling. "You have a big head. I'm sure you'll annoy me."

"As long as I keep you alive, does that matter?"

Liz moved next to him. "What are they saying?"

David relaxed. "They're getting to know each other. I think they're going to be fine together."

"Good. She's earned a break."

David finalized the arrangements with Dmitri. They would check into a modest hotel run by someone David trusted.

"You're going to have to lay low," he told the teenager. "No going out to meet your friends. We're talking about nine days in a hotel room. Can you handle that?"

"I don't want Kosanisky to find me. I will be very happy to stay inside." She tilted her head toward Dmitri. "He will go out for food?"

"Sure. Let him know if you want any books or magazines."

She fingered her oversize T-shirt. "I'll need some clothes."

"We'll get you some. You know you can't go back to your apartment. He'll have it watched."

Her expression tightened. "I have nothing there I need."

"Good. Now you two stay here until I get Liz and Natasha out of here."

Ten minutes later he urged Liz toward the door. He had Natasha in his arms, while Robert carried the car seat. When the car had been loaded, he started the engine but didn't shift gears.

Liz glanced at him. "What's the delay?"

He smiled. "You'll see."

Robert pulled out of his parking space and drove to the corner where he waited. A large garbage truck rumbled down from the other end of the street. David stayed in place until the truck was almost upon him, then he pulled out and headed for the corner. The garbage truck stayed on his bumper.

Liz looked over his shoulder, then back at him. "I'm guessing you arranged that?"

"It seemed like a good idea. Anyone lurking will have to get past the truck or go around. Either will offer a delay, which is what we want. Robert's going to hang back and see if we pick up a tail. We should be back at the apartment in about an hour."

David was true to his word. Sixty-five minutes later, Liz walked into the top-floor apartment and sighed in relief. Funny how this place had become so comfortable so quickly, she thought as she set down the diaper bag.

Natasha fussed as David carried her into the living room.

"I'm sure she's hungry," Liz said. "She probably needs changing, too."

"What's for dinner? Cereal and milk?"

"The menu won't be changing for a while."

He smiled. "Which end do you want to take care of?"

"I'll change her. You start dinner." She reached for the baby.

When she'd finished with diaper patrol, she carried

the little girl into the kitchen where she found David carefully stirring the cereal.

"The bottle is still heating," he said, pointing to the pot on the stove.

Liz settled herself in a chair and propped Natasha up in her arms. "Are you hungry?" she asked brightly. "Is my baby girl ready for dinner?"

Natasha waved her arms, then opened her mouth as David put the small bowl on the table.

"I'd say that's a yes," he said.

Liz used the baby spoon she'd brought with her and offered Natasha some cereal. She took it eagerly.

"How are you doing?" he asked Liz as he took a seat on the opposite site of the table. "Shaken?"

"As much as a James Bond martini," Liz admitted, focusing on the feeding because it was safer than thinking about the past few hours. "I'm glad Sophia is all right."

"It's good that you found her."

"Better me than someone else." She pictured the burn she'd seen and shuddered. "How can that man be so evil? It's wrong."

"He's in it for the money. To him this is just business."

"Can you stop him?"

"Right now I'm more concerned about keeping the three of you safe."

Safe. Did that mean alive? She wasn't sure she wanted to know.

She scooped up more cereal for Natasha. "Sophia

told me about her plans. She wants to go live in the country and marry a farmer she's never met."

"What are the odds of him being worse than what she's been through?"

Liz supposed he had a point, but she didn't like any of it. "She's seventeen. She told me started working for Kosanisky when she was fourteen. Where was her family in all this? Why wasn't there a place for her to go?"

"Kids fall through the cracks. It happens in American cities, too."

"I suppose." But they were statistics and Sophia was real. "I want to help her."

"You are."

"How? By taking her child away from her?"

"Yes." He leaned toward her. "You know she can't raise Natasha on her own."

"But if she's getting married…"

"Do you think there's a chance in hell she'll ever tell the guy the truth about her past? Why would she? He wouldn't want her then."

Which was pretty much what Sophia had said. "She wants to be a nice girl again. Leave all this behind."

"Which means leaving Natasha. If she has to give up her daughter, who better to take her?"

Liz stared at the baby in her lap. "There are too many hard choices in life."

"Always."

"These past few days have made me realize so much of what I worry about is really stupid and small. So what if I don't get a new account? No one is trying to kill me."

"Your problems are important to you."

She shook her head. "Not anymore. I'm not the same person I was. And when Natasha gets older, I'll tell her how brave and loving her mother was. How she sacrificed for her daughter."

"I'm sure Sophia would like that."

She finished feeding the baby, then held her up against her shoulder and walked her for a while. Night fell and with the darkness came the feeling of being cut off from the world. David's low voice soothed her as he made some phone calls. When the baby fell asleep in her arms, Liz longed for some rest of her own in a place that was less frightening and less strange.

Her heart ached for Sophia. No one should have to go through what she'd been through. Certainly not a teenager. Yet how many more victims existed in the city, the country, the world?

"I can't save them all," she whispered. But she could save one.

David came up behind her and took the baby from her. "It's getting late," he said. "Why don't you get ready for bed?"

"What are you going to do?"

"Ainsley is stopping by so I can bring her up to date on what's happening. We'll be quiet. Go on. You need to rest."

She felt both weary and drained. But sleep seemed impossible.

"I'll be right here," he promised.

As she nodded and walked to the bedroom, his words

sank into her heart. She absorbed them and made them a part of her being, realizing that she wanted them to be true for always.

How was that possible? She didn't want close connections. She feared love brought death. Or she had.

Suddenly what her parents had done seemed like a lifetime ago. She wasn't them, she hadn't lived their lives. Today she'd heard of horrors that would haunt her for years. She'd seen bruises and burn marks. She'd sensed the evil in the world.

Perhaps the only way to combat it was with light and goodness. And love.

She glanced over her shoulder and watched as David gently rocked Natasha in his arms. He held her with a confidence that spoke of practice and caring. Liz could imagine him holding other children. Their children? Was she going to turn her back on who this man was because her mother had died of a broken heart?

What a waste of a life, she thought sadly. Her mother could have lived for her child, for the memory of the man she'd loved. Instead she'd given up without trying.

"I'm not like her," Liz whispered as she walked into the bedroom. "I'm not like her at all."

David let Ainsley in shortly after ten.

"How's it going?" she asked as she shrugged out of her jacket. "Robert filled me in on some of what happened today. What a nightmare for Sophia. He says she's just a kid."

"Seventeen."

Ainsley pushed her blond hair off her shoulders and walked to the sofa. "That bastard. I'd like to catch Kosanisky myself."

David waited while she pulled files out of her briefcase.

"What do you know about him?" he asked when she was settled.

"Plenty. If there's money to be made, he's into it. Plenty of black market imports even before it was popular. Prostitution, gambling. If there's a vice to be exploited, he's the man."

She leaned forward and poured herself a cup of coffee from the pot he'd left on the table.

"Can we find him?" he asked.

"I don't know. That depends on his resources. The more people he has working for him the more layers of protection between us and him. But all those employees also make him vulnerable. We only have to find one to crack."

"Do we have one?"

"I should know in a few days."

David wasn't sure they had that long. "Can you work faster?"

"I'll do my best." She sipped her coffee. "How's Liz holding up?"

"As well as can be expected. This is more than she signed on for. She's upset. Restless."

"I'm sure she wants to be gone," Ainsley said sympathetically. "I see you have a team downstairs."

"Rotating shifts," he agreed. "I've arranged for a safe house if this place gets made, but I'm hoping we won't have to use it."

Better for Liz if they could stay in one place.

He and Ainsley talked business for another half an hour. When she left, he bolted the door behind her and set the sophisticated alarm. Then he walked through the apartment to make sure everything was secure.

Natasha slept soundly in her crib. She'd kicked off her blanket so he pulled it over her and lightly stroked her head.

Liz lay on one side of the large bed, her face turned away, her body curved. He wanted to touch her, as well, but instead continued to check the windows.

In the dining room he spotted a thick pad under some magazines. He made sure the drapes were pulled shut all the way, then clicked on a lamp and pulled out the pad.

The oversize pages were covered with quick sketches. He immediately recognized Liz's style and talent. There were drawings of a house he guessed to be her own and a small mixed-breed dog. About halfway in were several drawings of Natasha.

She'd captured the curve of the baby's cheeks, the plumpness of her fingers. With just a few strokes of a pencil she caught a smile, a wave, a bounce.

He brushed his fingers over the drawing, rubbing gently as if touching the artist herself. He ached for her as he'd never ached for anyone before. Need grew—not just for sex but for something more. He'd never considered himself a likely candidate for that kind of a relationship. There were too many flaws, too many dark places. Good sense said he should let Liz go.

But for once he didn't want to be sensible or even smart. He wanted to lay claim to her and this child. He wanted them to be his, and he theirs.

Black and white, he thought as he looked at the amazing drawings. Shades of gray—much like his world would be when she and the baby were gone.

Thirteen

Liz bent over her sketch pad and drew as quickly as she could. David sat in a pool of sunlight, Natasha in his arms. He held a bottle, while the baby fed and stared at him. His lips were curved in a smile, and her body relaxed into his.

"It's perfect," she murmured, delighted to be capturing the moment. "I'm nearly done."

"I looked at your pictures last night," he said. "You're even more amazing than you were five years ago."

She looked up and grinned. "Lots of practice."

"Is that what it is?"

"Uh-huh. I've been working hard."

"Will you do anything with these sketches? Have a showing or something?"

"No. They're just for me. You're welcome to pick out a few if you'd like them."

As soon as she made the offer, she winced silently. Maybe David was just being kind about her drawings.

"I'd like that a lot," he told her. "Can you draw one of yourself?"

She looked up so suddenly, she nearly fell off her

chair. His dark gaze settled on her face, warming her with intimate attention.

"I've never done a self portrait."

"You should try. The subject is beautiful."

"David!" She felt herself flushing.

Something was different. Despite the danger, despite the tension and the uncertainty, she felt as if she and David had turned an emotional corner somewhere. The sexual awareness lurked in the background, but somehow it had grown fuller, richer. She didn't just want to be with him in bed—she wanted much, much more.

"Did you have to put a lot of work on hold to come to Moscow?" he asked.

"A few projects, but once I'd made the first visit, I knew the second one was coming. I was able to reschedule things fairly easily. The clients I told were extremely supportive."

"What happens when you get home? Will you be taking Natasha into work with you?"

"I wish, but I think she would be too much of a distraction." She set down her pencil. "Actually, I'm joining up with another graphics firm. We're combining resources moving from our smaller individual offices to a larger joint office." She set down the pad and pencil. "This will scare you. Three women working together. Does the thought of it make you want to turn on sports?"

"A little," he admitted as he adjusted the bottle. "What's the appeal for you?"

"We all have families. Our goal is to have successful careers *and* time at home. We're going to each work three days a week. I'll be working at home some for the first few months, while Natasha is adjusting. I've arranged for a fabulous baby-sitter. Actually I found her through Children's Connection. She's a former nurse who retired and is doing part-time day care. So that's great."

"You have it all planned out."

"I did my best. I'm sure there will be plenty of unexpected crises, but I'll handle them."

She wouldn't have a choice. Natasha would only have her to depend on.

"Enough about me," she said. "What about you? How long are you going to hide out in the wilds of Moscow?"

"Good question."

"Do you have an equally excellent answer?"

Natasha finished the bottle. David put it on the coffee table, then carefully shifted her onto his shoulder and patted her back.

"I've enjoyed my time here," he said. "The work has been interesting."

"Yeah, so interesting you can't talk about it."

"Exactly. I know I've made a difference and that matters."

She tilted her head. "Not to be too nosy, but aren't you rich?"

Natasha burped loudly.

"She wants to know, too," Liz told him.

David chuckled. "The Logan family is well-off."

"And as you're a member..."

"I'm well-off, too."

"So you don't have to work?" she asked.

"Probably not."

"That's something you should actually know." She leaned forward. "It's not that you're rich that's so interesting, it's that you don't have to work, yet you've chosen a difficult and dangerous profession, and you're interested in a job that lets you make a difference. That says something about who you are."

"In a good way?" he asked humorously.

She thought about all he'd done for her and Natasha. How even now he protected them. "In the best way possible."

Tension crackled between them. Liz wasn't sure what it meant and it made her more than a little nervous. She decided a change in subject would help.

"So, if you did leave Moscow, would you continue to work for the government?"

"I'm not sure. I have an open invitation to go into the family computer business in Portland."

That startled her. Then questions filled her brain. Did he want to? Would he ever? Would he now?

"Interesting," she said, going for light and afraid she just sounded strangled. "So, um, with all that going for you, why isn't there a Mrs. David in the picture?"

"I'm not the marrying kind."

She laughed, then pointed at the baby in his arms. "All evidence to the contrary, right?"

"Okay." He grinned sheepishly. "I like Natasha. But this is temporary. Marriage is forever."

"Which you don't like?"

"Who would want me?"

She blinked...twice. "Excuse me? You're smart, funny, caring, great in a crisis, successful and rich. What's not to like?"

"Maybe I should have you design a business card for me."

"Do you need the help?"

He rose and carried Natasha to her. She took the baby and he crossed to a sideboard and braced his hands on the top. "I've told you about my past. How I spent the first few years."

"Sure, but what does that have to do with anything?"

He glanced at her over his shoulder. "Liz, I couldn't speak normally until I was five. I was ten before I could read. I went all through school with a learning disability."

"I don't want to dismiss your effort, but so what? Everyone overcomes something. From where I'm sitting, all you've been through means you worked your butt off and you have great character. Neither of those are characteristics women run from."

"This is different."

She couldn't believe what he was saying. "Do you think there's something fundamentally wrong with you? Is that what this is about?"

He shrugged. "Maybe."

She stood. The baby cooed and gurgled happily.

"David, you are what you've made yourself. I think you're amazing. I think—"

An explosion of glass cut her off in midsentence. Liz had no idea what was going on, but David lunged for her. He grabbed the baby from her arms and roughly pushed Liz to the carpet.

"Get down," he yelled. "Get down now!"

"What?"

She collapsed onto the floor. The air rushed from her lungs.

More crashes echoed in the room. After a second she realized they were being shot at.

"No!" she gasped.

She glanced around frantically. David held Natasha against his chest. He'd curled his body around her, using himself as a shield. She cried in protest.

"Liz, are you all right?" he demanded. "Are you shot?"

"I'm okay." She wasn't sure, but nothing hurt.

"We have to get out of here. They may have men in the building. I don't know. They're shooting from across the street."

Half sliding, half crawling, he made his way to the wall with the window, then inched across the floor. Liz saw right away that sliding under the window meant he couldn't be seen by the shooter. She followed.

They made it to the bedroom. There were no more shots, but Natasha continued to cry loudly. David handed her over, then stood and opened a security panel. He punched in a code.

"I've activated the team," he said. "They'll be here in less than two minutes. Don't move."

There was a large armoire by the window. He stood next to it and pulled open the doors. After jerking out the contents, he leaned his weight against it and slowly pushed it across the floor so it covered the window.

"Okay, now," he said tersely, "get what you need for her for a couple of days. Diapers, food, change of clothing. Make sure you have your passport, your plane ticket and your wallet. You have two minutes."

Then he was gone. Liz jumped when she heard another shot from the other room. Every cell in her body trembled. She couldn't breathe and didn't know what to do.

This couldn't be happening, she thought. It wasn't possible. People like her didn't get shot at.

Natasha continued to cry. Finally, Liz forced herself to think. What had David said? They were leaving. She had to get herself together.

"Formula, diapers, clothes," she muttered. "Wallet, passport, tickets."

She put the screaming infant into the car seat and quickly fastened her.

"I'm sorry," she whispered as the baby squirmed in protest. "I need you safe."

She put the car seat on the floor, so the bed was between Natasha and the window. If a bullet got through the armoire, she didn't want it hitting her child.

Feeling returned to her arms and legs, which only made her shake more. She forced the fear away and concentrated on gathering supplies. Fortunately, she kept the baby's things together. She dropped what she needed into the diaper bag, then checked the contents of her purse. When David walked back into the room, she had just finished shoving her arms into a sweater.

"I'm done," she said.

"Let's move."

She turned to pick up Natasha and nearly screamed when she saw the gun in David's hand. Just as frightening, he looked as if he knew how to use it. She picked up the diaper bag and slung it over her shoulder, while he took the car seat.

Two men waited at the front door of the apartment. Mrs. P. hovered in the hallway.

"Go," the old woman said. "Go quickly."

Liz followed David. One man went in front of them, one followed behind.

"Ziegler is in the stairwell," the first man said. "He says it's clear."

As they raced down the stairs, Liz stumbled a couple of times but kept going. David moved with a sureness she envied. Natasha continued to cry, the sound echoing in the stairwell.

In the basement they ran through the tunnel linking the building with the underground parking garage.

"They could have made my car," David said. "Give me your keys."

One of the men tossed him keys.

"Activate the safe house," he told them. "When we get away, call Ainsley and tell her what's happened. I'll be in touch when I can."

David steered her toward a blue Opal. Liz jerked open the back door and reached for the car seat.

"You'll have to secure her while I'm driving," he said, and pushed her inside. He shoved Natasha in after her and slammed the door shut.

Seconds later he was behind the wheel and they were peeling out of the garage.

Liz worked frantically. She snapped the car seat into place, then reached for her own seat belt.

"Get down," David yelled as they tore out of the structure. A millisecond later the passenger window exploded.

Liz screamed and threw herself on top of Natasha. The baby screamed louder. David swore. Liz had never been so terrified in her life. She wasn't sure how it was possible to feel so much fear and still live.

The car swerved left, then right. The violent movement made her wonder if David had been hit. She looked up, but couldn't see any blood.

"Get down," he told her again, his voice tight with tension.

"I have to protect Natasha."

"You're no good to her dead."

She knew he was right, but she couldn't save herself and leave the baby exposed. She stayed draped over the car seat.

They turned and sped and swerved until she started to feel nauseated. Finally, David slowed a little, and she straightened.

"Did we lose them?"

"I hope so."

He turned into a parking lot, pulling up to a white

car. As he grabbed the diaper bag and stepped out on his side, the man driving the white car stepped out, as well. He reached for Liz's door.

"It's all right," David told her as he circled the vehicle. "Hurry."

She unfastened Natasha and passed her over, then collected her purse and got out of the car.

Her legs shook so much she could barely walk, yet she forced herself to take the three steps to the white car and slide into the back seat. Once again she had to fasten Natasha in place while David took off out of the parking lot.

They drove for what felt like hours. There were two more car switches, including one where they only pretended to change vehicles. Finally, shortly before sunset, they pulled onto a quiet street lined with brownstones. He drove to the fourth one down, hit a remote control on the visor, then waited while a garage door slowly opened.

"Where are we?" she asked.

"A safe house. Don't worry. We weren't followed."

"How do you know?"

"Because a team of my men have been tailing us for the past two hours. They would have warned me if there was a problem."

David drove into the garage and closed the door behind them. He helped her carry Natasha inside, along with the diaper bag.

The house was narrow, long and three stories high. Liz was surprised to find food in the refrigerator, a crib in one of the bedrooms and toiletries in the bathroom.

"So the safe house comes furnished," she said with a casualness she didn't feel.

"It makes life easier."

Natasha still cried. Liz got her out of the car seat and held her in her arms.

"I'm sorry," she murmured to the baby. "This has been horrible for you. It's all right now, sweetie. You're safe."

She looked at David who had pulled out a cell phone. "We are safe, right?"

He nodded. "For now. But this has to stop."

"I like that plan." She kissed the baby's forehead, then turned back to him. "What about Sophia? Is she all right?"

"She should be, but I'll check to make sure. Then I need to call home."

Maybe she'd hit herself on the head and hadn't realized it. "You need to *what?*"

"Call Portland. I want to talk to my father."

"Okay. Why?"

"Because we can't go on like this. I'm calling in a few favors."

"Which means?"

"My father is a powerful man. He'll take this right to the top."

Her stomach lurched. "And who's at the top?"

"The president."

Liz paced in the hallway while David made calls. After polishing off cereal and a bottle, Natasha had dozed off. It was good that one of them could rest. Liz had the feeling that she would never be caught up on sleep again.

A thousand different images whirled through her mind. David helping her. Their mad car dash through the city. Her terror when bullets had crashed into the apartment. Who were the men after her baby and how were they to be stopped? And did David's father really know the president of the United States?

Nearly an hour later David stepped out of the house's small library and smiled. "It's done."

"Meaning?"

"The judge has agreed to move up the hearing to tomorrow. You don't have to wait the full ten days."

"That's great," she said with relief. "Will I be able to take her home with me after the hearing?"

"On the midnight flight. I'll take you from the hearing to the embassy, and then you're on your way."

She opened her mouth, then closed it. Home. As in away from David. Funny how the ache in her heart was just as powerful as the fear had been.

Of course she wanted to be gone, but she wasn't ready to leave David—not yet. There was so much she wanted to say to him. There were things she wanted to hear. Was he ready to move back to the States? Did she matter to him? Had their relationship been the result of the danger they faced, or was there something else? They'd both felt something five years ago, which to her mind was still alive and well, but did he agree with her?

"We would like to use the hearing as a setup to get the men after you," he said.

She had to take a second to switch mental gears. "You want to capture them?"

"As many as we can." He moved close. "You don't have to do this, Liz. I won't deny there's an element of danger. But if you're willing to help, I swear I'll protect you with my life."

His dark eyes glowed with conviction and something else. An emotion she wanted to name as love, but she wasn't sure. How did he feel about her? How did she feel about him?

"I trust you," she said.

He leaned forward and kissed her. "You won't regret it."

Any hopes Liz had for a quiet, romantic evening were quickly dashed when David's "team" showed up to plan the sting. She made herself useful getting coffee and making sandwiches and sat in on their meeting for a while, but eventually she didn't want to hear any more so she retreated upstairs.

After rolling Natasha's crib into the main bedroom, she curled up on the mattress and watched the little girl sleep. Her own eyes felt gritty and swollen, but she couldn't seem to relax enough to doze off.

Sometime after two in the morning, Ainsley knocked lightly on the door.

"I came to check on you," the woman said. "I know this can be a bit overwhelming."

Liz sat up. "I'm okay."

The pretty blonde moved to the crib and smiled at the sleeping baby. "She's amazing."

"I know."

"She's not going to be in any danger."

Liz had determined that much from what she'd heard. Still, she couldn't help worrying. "What if they figure out what we're doing?"

"They won't."

Good words, but they didn't make her feel any better.

Ainsley moved closer and sat on the edge of the bed. "Don't worry. David would never let anything happen to either of you." Her smile turned rueful. "It's nice to finally know the reason after all this time."

"The reason for what?"

Ainsley sighed. "I've had a thing for my boss since the day he reported here five years ago, and he never looked at me twice. He dated some, but only casually. No one seemed to touch his heart. I couldn't figure out why until you showed up."

Liz felt her cheeks flushing. "I wasn't the reason."

"Weren't you? I was at that party. The one you came to your first night here. I saw him waiting for you to arrive and I saw his face when he first spotted you. I would say the man has it bad." She stood. "He's one of the good guys. You're very lucky. I keep telling myself there's someone just as wonderful waiting for me. I just have to find him."

"You will," Liz promised, although she wasn't sure what she was saying. Was Ainsley right? Was she the reason David had never gotten involved with anyone? Had their time together five years ago touched him as much as it had touched her?

The possibilities gave her hope and the determination to find out the truth. But first she had to get through the hearing the next day.

Liz woke up to more rain. Once again the gray skies and wet world suited her mood. Terror and apprehension made it impossible to eat, and when they left for the hearing, she couldn't stop shaking.

David didn't say much as they drove through Moscow. She knew about the cars tailing them, about the security agents already in place in the old building. She knew where Ainsley was and what she was doing, and still Liz couldn't seem to catch her breath.

"How are you holding up?" David asked.

She had to swallow before speaking. "Okay, I guess."

He chuckled. "You're still not a very good liar."

There was so much she needed to say to him, but this wasn't the time. Not with so much on the line.

She shifted in her seat. She was both hot and cold and the bulletproof vest she wore made her uncomfortable. Nothing felt real or right and all she wanted was to be home right now. Home with her baby and safe.

They arrived more quickly than she would have thought. There were people on the sidewalk and in front of the building. Regular citizens? she wondered. Or the enemy?

David helped her with the baby then wrapped his arm around her as he hurried her toward the front entrance. There seemed to be a thousand people watching them, waiting for the right moment. When would they attack?

By the time they reached the hearing room, Liz was barely breathing. Her heart pounded so hard, she felt sure it must be bruised. The trembling made it difficult to walk, and the baby in her arms seemed to weigh a hundred pounds.

There were people everywhere. She tried to remember if there were more than when she'd had her first hearing, but she couldn't recall.

She wanted to tell David she couldn't do this. That she wasn't strong or capable. She wanted to crumple into a ball on the floor and surrender. Instead she moved toward the table at the far end of the room.

Their footsteps were loud in the silence, which meant the sudden cocking of a gun echoed like thunder.

"You will stop right there," a man said in a thick accent.

Liz froze. David stayed at her side as they both turned to find a tall, thin man pointing a gun at them.

"You will give me the baby."

Liz nodded and held out her arms. The man reached toward the bundle. Then she stepped back and somehow the baby was falling and falling until it hit the floor. The man stared down in horror.

Doors burst open from all sides of the room.

"Don't move," someone called loudly, then said something in Russian. Liz assumed it was the same command.

Agents poured into the hearing room, and the would-be kidnapper dropped his gun.

While David grabbed his weapon, agents arrested everyone in the room. Liz dropped to her knees and pushed the blankets away from the doll she'd been holding. At the same time she reached in her jacket pocket for the cell phone David had given her and punched in the number she'd memorized.

"It's done," she said.

"Good," Ainsley told her. "Natasha and I are waiting with the judge whenever you're ready."

Fourteen

Liz had never been so happy to see an American flag in her life. She nearly wept when the marine guarding the American embassy opened her car door, and it was all she could do not to hug him.

"She's here?" she asked David for the thousandth time. "In the embassy? The judge said—"

"It's okay," he promised, taking her hand and walking her inside. "We had a talk with the judge and while he's not willing to give us any names, he came here to grant you full custody of Natasha."

They walked through high-ceilinged rooms and down corridors until they came into a large open area. Liz saw the judge and Ainsley, but she wasn't prepared for who held Natasha.

"You are well?" Sophia asked.

Liz nodded. "How about you?"

"I am healing."

Liz stared at the baby in her mother's arms. She could see the resemblance between them and her heart began to break.

"Sophia," she said, but the teenager cut her off.

"No. This is right. From here I go to the train. Mr. Logan has arranged it."

"Dmitri will take her," David said.

Liz took in the girl's steady gaze. Her bruises were fading, her scrapes healing, but there was still pain in her eyes.

"I could sponsor you," Liz said. "You could come with me to Oregon. Portland is very beautiful. Once you settled in, you could go to college, be anything you want."

The teenager kissed her daughter's cheek, then passed her to Liz.

"No. This is where I belong. I am Russian."

The judge stepped forward and said something in Russian. Maggie Sullivan, the social worker, burst into the room.

"Sorry," she said breathlessly. "I got caught in traffic."

She handed the judge the paperwork and he carefully looked it over. Then he signed the documents and nodded.

"She yours now," he said in broken English.

"Thank you," Liz said.

Ainsley patted her back. "We're already working on Natasha's visa. You'll be on the midnight flight."

Liz couldn't believe it. Was this really happening, after all she'd been through? Was it possible?

She looked at all the people who had helped her. Dmitri, Maggie, Ainsley, Sophia and David. Tears filled her eyes.

She held out her free arm to Sophia, who moved close and hugged her. Maggie and Ainsley stepped in. Then Liz felt David's warm embrace.

"You're going home," he said into her ear. "You're going to be where you belong."

Vladimir Kosanisky paced the length of his office. He stared at the phone, willing it to ring, and when it did, he didn't want to answer it.

"Da," he said when he finally picked it up. "Kosanisky."

"I heard what happened," a familiar American voice said. "You failed."

"There were too many of them. The baby was not with them. They had already taken her to the embassy."

"How many of your men did they capture?"

"Five. My men will not talk. The Americans let the judge go, but he is of no use to us now." Kosanisky swallowed when he'd finished. He knew the price of failing.

There were several seconds of silence. They spun longer and longer, all the while Kosanisky imagined various ways the Stork would have him killed.

"I'll contact our clients," the American said at last. "Tell them that there's a problem with this child. We will find another for them."

Sweet relief filled Kosanisky's chest and made it easier to breathe. So he wasn't going to have to hunt down Sophia's bastard. Good. Let the American woman have her.

"Yes," he agreed. "Another child would be better. I will start the search immediately."

"See that you don't make another mistake," the Stork told him. "Next time I won't be so understanding."

There was a click as the line was disconnected. Kosanisky replaced the receiver and tried to ignore the cold chill on the back of his neck. The one that told him this was his last chance to get it right.

David brought Liz's suitcases to her. He'd sent one of his men to his apartment to collect her things.

She sat with Natasha in a large chair by the window. It was after six. Mother and child would be leaving for the airport in a few hours. The ticking clock reminded him of another evening when one of them was going away. Five years ago he hadn't been willing to take a chance. What about now?

"How are you feeling?" he asked as he crossed to the chair next to hers.

"Numb," she admitted. "I can't believe it's over."

"It is. She's yours. As soon as you pass through immigration in the States, Natasha becomes an American citizen."

Liz smiled at the little girl. "We're hanging up a flag in front of the house as soon as we get home."

He took her free hand in his. "Tell me about your house."

"It's two stories. On the Willamette River. The people who had the house built were relocated to the east coast before construction was finished, so I got to pick things like floor covering and appliances." She smiled. "I can't really afford it, but I love it so much, I don't mind. There's a huge open room over the garage. I had big windows installed on the south wall, so I get the best light. That's where I work when I'm not at the office."

He rubbed his thumb across the back of her hand. Her skin was smooth and warm. Desire coiled through him, but there was also something else. Something powerful and permanent. He hadn't recognized it five years ago, but he knew it now.

"I'm coming home," he said quietly. "I've done what I came to do." He looked into her eyes. "You're not the reason I'm leaving, although you've helped me see what I want and what's important."

Her mouth parted slightly but she'd didn't speak. Hope filled her eyes, which warmed his heart.

"I carry my past with me," he continued. "I can't escape what I was."

"You shouldn't want to. It's made you who you are. An amazing man."

He smiled. "You always see the best in me."

"I see what's there."

"Then do you see the empty place, Liz? Do you see the loneliness? Do you see how much I love you? Because I do. More than anything."

Liz squeezed his fingers as pure joy bubbled through her. "I love you, too," she whispered. "Oh, David, I desperately wanted to leave, but I didn't want to be apart from you. Our time together has only confirmed what I suspected when we met five years ago."

He brought her hand to his mouth and kissed her knuckles, then leaned forward and kissed her mouth.

"Five years ago you wanted to come with me," he

said. "Now it's my turn to say, 'let me accompany you on your journey. Let me share your adventure.' Marry me, Liz. Marry me and let me be your husband and Natasha's father."

She felt tears on her cheeks. "Yes! Yes, please. I want us to be together. To be a family. To have children together."

"Do you think Natasha would like some brothers and sisters?"

"Absolutely."

He wrapped his arms around her and squeezed. Natasha woke with a cry of protest and he leaned back with a laugh.

"Sorry, kid," he said as he collected the baby.

Liz watched his easy movements, how comfortably he held the little girl, and knew everything about this moment was right.

He stood and motioned to the door. "Come and help me pack," he said. "I have a plane to catch."

She moved close to him. "I hope there's an empty seat on the midnight flight."

He pulled a ticket out of his pocket. "Funny you should mention that."

She laughed. He wrapped his free arm around her and she leaned into him. They both held Natasha. Maybe it had taken that time apart for them to see what was really important. Maybe they both had to risk everything to find their way home. They'd found it now and Liz knew that was all that mattered.

*Turn the page for a sneak preview of the
next emotional
LOGAN'S LEGACY title,
SECRETS & SEDUCTIONS*

*by veteran author Pamela Toth
on sale in July 2004...*

One

"Ms. Wright? I'm Morgan Davis." He extended his hand, his grip warm and firm. "Won't you come in and have a seat?"

He nodded to the receptionist, who shut the door quietly behind her. Emma took one of the purple tub chairs in front of the desk and the tall windows. Willing herself to be calm, she took a deep, slow breath.

Instead of returning to his black leather throne, the director surprised her by sitting in the chair facing hers. He was startlingly attractive, with deep blue eyes and cheekbones that would make a photographer weep. His dark tan was emphasized by his white shirt and maroon tie.

Ignoring the awareness dancing across her nerves, Emma stayed focused on her mission. She glanced over at the folder lying open on the desktop behind him. Did it contain the information she had come here to find?

He turned his head for a moment. His profile should have been on a stamp. His jaw was strong, his nose straight and his black eyelashes were as thick as the bristles of a paintbrush. Before she reeled herself back in, Emma wondered if the honey-gold tan of his face and hands extended to the rest of him.

"How can I help you?" he asked, lifting his brows.

Emma crossed her legs, trying not to fidget, and moistened her suddenly dry lips. She'd planned so carefully what she wanted to say, but now her mind threatened to go blank.

"I just found out that your agency handled my adoption," she finally blurted, lacing her fingers together tightly. "Is that my file on your desk?"

"That's right," he replied without turning his head. "As you can imagine, our records go back many years." He folded his arms loosely across his chest. His smile flashed even white teeth. "I hope there isn't a problem."

Sitting rigidly, she lifted her chin. The sense of injustice and pain still raged inside her. "The problem is that I wasn't told about it until a very short time ago."

He frowned, clearly puzzled. "About this agency?"

"About being adopted," she clarified. "I had no idea until now."

His expression softened as he leaned forward. "I'm so sorry." His voice was husky. "After all this time, the news must have come as quite a shock. I expect it's been difficult for you."

"Yes, very." She pressed her lips together to keep them from trembling. Her voice wobbled. "That's why I'm here, to find out what I can."

His frown returned. "I'll help in any way that I can,

of course," he replied, "but I'm not sure what you're asking."

"I need the names of my biological parents," she said firmly. The Wrights had claimed not to have that information, but her faith in their honesty had taken a major hit and she wasn't sure that she believed them.

"If you don't mind my asking, how did this all come about?" He spread his hands wide. "After keeping your adoption a secret for all this time, what made them suddenly decide to tell you, do you know?"

His sympathetic smile and his show of interest threatened to shatter Emma's composure. Afraid she might break down and start sobbing, she clenched her teeth and stared down at her toes, painted red to match her shirt.

Deliberately, Emma stiffened her spine. "I found out just recently that I have a medical condition which is usually considered to be hereditary," she began.

His eyes narrowed with concern. "I hope it's nothing serious."

"Well, I'm not dying or anything like that," she said quickly.

He made a noncommittal murmur of relief.

"It's just that when I talked to my parents—" Emma shook her head and corrected herself "—my adoptive parents, it became obvious that I didn't inherit it from either side of the family."

Emma swallowed the bitter taste of regret. "Sometimes I wish that I had let the subject drop, but I can't go back, can I?" she asked the man seated across from her.

"If that were possible, I'm sure there are things in all our lives that we would change."

Was that sadness she heard in his deep voice or merely empathy? With his looks and his position of authority here, plus whatever else he had going, did he still have regrets?

"What did you do after that?" he prompted her gently.

"I did some research on the Web," she admitted grimly, "and then I hotfooted it back to my parents' house with a couple of real burning questions."

"The Internet may not be the best place to get medical information," he reminded her. "There can be many different ways to interpret whatever you might find there."

"Oh, I know." Emma had been bluffing when she brought the subject up again. "I tried not to jump to any conclusions, but there was a look that passed between my parents—"

This time she didn't bother to correct herself as she bowed her head. The habit of more than a quarter of a century wasn't going to be changed in a matter of weeks, no matter the sense of betrayal burning in her heart.

"Anyway," she continued, blinking hard, "a red flag went up and I just knew." She looked back at him. "At first they denied everything, but I kept pushing. Finally the whole sordid story came out."

Since he'd read Emma's file, he knew more about her right now than she did. "Are you sure that it's sordid?" he asked.

"That's what I'm to find out."

His expression changed, becoming more wary. "What do you mean?"

Emma rolled her eyes. "After the big confession, they actually expected me to accept their apology, let the subject drop, to go on as though nothing was any different." She waved her hand in a gesture of dismissal. "But of course I can't do that."

It had been painfully clear to her that her *adoptive* parents had never intended telling her the truth at all. Thank God the subject was no longer shrouded in secrecy.

"So that's why I've come to you." Emma gave him what she hoped to be a beguiling smile. "I'm here to find out about my real parents."

"I'm sorry, but what you're asking is impossible. This agency can't help you."

* * * * *

"Joanna Wayne weaves together a romance and suspense
with pulse-pounding results!"
—*New York Times* bestselling author Tess Gerritsen

National bestselling author

JOANNA WAYNE

Alligator Moon

Determined to find his brother's killer, John Robicheaux finds
himself entangled with investigative reporter Callie Havelin.
Together they must shadow the sinister killer slithering in the
murky waters—before they are consumed by the darkness....

A riveting tale that shouldn't be missed!

Coming in June 2004.

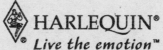